BREAKING THE PLAYBOY'S RULES

BY
EMILY FORBES

MILLS & BOON

First published in Great Britain 2013
by Mills & Boon, an imprint of Harlequin (UK) Limited.
Harlequin (UK) Limited, Eton House,
18-24 Paradise Road, Richmond, Surrey TW9 1SR

© Emily Forbes 2013

ISBN: 978 0 263 89873 6

Harlequin (UK) policy is to use papers that are natural, renewable and recyclable products and made from wood grown in sustainable forests. The logging and manufacturing process conform to the legal environmental regulations of the country of origin.

Printed and bound in Spain
by Blackprint CPI, Barcelona

Emily Forbes began her writing life as a partnership between two sisters who are both passionate bibliophiles. As a team Emily had ten books published, and one of her proudest moments was when her tenth book was nominated for the 2010 Australian Romantic Book of the Year Award.

While Emily's love of writing remains as strong as ever, the demands of life with young families has recently made it difficult to work on stories together. But rather than give up her dream Emily now writes solo. The challenges may be different, but the reward of having a book published is still as sweet as ever.

Whether as a team or as an individual Emily hopes to keep bringing stories to her readers. Her inspiration comes from everywhere, and stories she hears while travelling, at mothers' lunches, in the media and in her other career as a physiotherapist all get embellished with a large dose of imagination until they develop a life of their own.

If you would like to get in touch with Emily you can e-mail her at emilyforbes@internode.on.net

Recent titles by the same author:

SYDNEY HARBOUR HOSPITAL: BELLA'S WISHLIST*
GEORGIE'S BIG GREEK WEDDING?
BREAKING HER NO-DATES RULE
NAVY OFFICER TO FAMILY MAN
DR DROP-DEAD-GORGEOUS
THE PLAYBOY FIREFIGHTER'S PROPOSAL

Sydney Harbour Hospital

For my Mum, Barbara, and my mother-in-law, Tess,
both of whom dreamt of working
on Outback stations—it's not too late!

And for Michelle, an English ex-pat
who came to Australia on a working visa, fell in love,
and now lives on a cattle station on the Cooper Creek
in Outback Queensland with Jon and their four boys—
including my godson Keegan.

CHAPTER ONE

Emma!
When are you coming to visit? You know I'm seri-
ous—I'm actually taking time to sit down and write!!!

Use some of your inheritance and get your butt
on a plane. You can hang in Sydney with the olds
until you get over your jet lag and then fly out to me.
You'll love it out here—remember when we were
teenagers and you loved everything Australian? Do
you remember watching that television series about
the flying doctors? (How could you forget—you took
all the videos back to England with you☺!) Well, this
is where the real ones are! Come on, you HAVE to
come and visit.

I promise you, the minute you see the Outback
and I introduce you to some real Aussie men you'll
forget all your worries. It'll give you a chance to get
some distance and perspective and get what's-his-
name OUT OF YOUR SYSTEM!!!!

Don't think about it, Em, just do it!
See you soon,
Love, Soph xx

SOPHIE's letter read exactly the way she talked and lived.
Her words, like her speech, were peppered with exclama-

tion marks. Everything she did she did quickly and with passion. She never seemed to stop and her enthusiasm had been the prompt that had got Emma on this plane. Without Sophie's cajoling Emma knew she'd still be sitting in England, feeling depressed and wondering if she could really make this trip on her own. Without Sophie's insistence she might not have booked her ticket. But now she was almost there.

Emma folded the letter and slid it back into its envelope, taking care not to tear the paper. She'd read it every day for the past month and it was beginning to show signs of wear but even though she knew the words verbatim she couldn't bring herself to put it away permanently.

Sophie's letter wasn't the reason she'd packed her bags and said farewell to her stepmother and half-sisters in order to fly halfway around the world but it had been the catalyst. Emma needed the letter. It was her anchor. It kept her tethered to reality. It helped to make this whole adventure seem real—even when she could scarcely believe she had actually made it Down Under.

Thinking back to the events that had led her here was upsetting so she focussed again on the landscape beneath her as she tried to think of happier, more positive things. But as she looked out the window at this strange land she felt a trace of unease. She'd had a few moments of trepidation over the past month, although not as many as most people seemed to expect her to have, but looking at the vast, dry, red land beneath the plane's wings she questioned the wisdom of leaving the familiarity of England to fly to the middle of nowhere.

But you were miserable in England, she reminded herself.

Yes, but you might still be miserable here.

At this point she wasn't sure which was preferable—

being miserable in familiar surroundings or being miserable in a strange, new world. She hoped Sophie was right and a change of scenery would keep her too occupied to notice she was miserable. Sophie had promised her that it was hard to be depressed in a place where the sun was almost always shining, and because Emma had long wanted to come back to Australia she chose to believe her. And now she was here. Almost.

As Emma felt the plane start to descend she slipped the envelope between the pages of the novel she was reading and stowed it in her handbag. She took a deep breath. It was too late to turn back now. She let her breath out with a long sigh.

'Are you okay?'

It took Emma a moment to realise the girl in the seat beside her was talking to her. And another moment to realise she was asking because she'd sighed out loud.

She turned to face her. They hadn't spoken to each other during the flight; they'd smiled a greeting when they'd first sat down but then Emma had pulled her book from her bag and started reading. She didn't like striking up conversations with fellow travellers as there was always the danger that they'd talk non-stop for the entire trip and Emma then found it difficult to politely excuse herself from the contact. But looking at her now she wondered if she'd seemed rude. The girl was about the same age as her, in her mid-twenties, and she did look genuinely concerned.

'Yes, I'm fine, thanks,' she replied. 'Just thinking.'

'You're English?'

Emma nodded.

'Are you here on holiday or for work?'

Emma wasn't really sure how to describe her visit. She wanted to make herself believe it was a holiday, although it felt more like an escape. She knew she was running away from her old life, just temporarily, but she didn't want to admit that out loud. Not to a stranger, not even to herself. 'I'm visiting family,' she said. That was the truth, even if it wasn't the whole truth.

'Are you staying long?'

'I'm not sure yet,' she replied. She hadn't planned any further ahead than getting to Broken Hill. Her life tended to move in cycles and she'd found, on more than one occasion, that things seemed to happen without her input. Sometimes she was happy with the way events unfolded, sometimes not, but she had always had a sense that there were some things she couldn't control so sometimes she didn't bother trying. More often than not, too, her plans, when she did make them, went awry so she avoided making them whenever she could. Right now her only goal was to get to Broken Hill. Once she was there there'd be time enough to work out what she was going to do next.

Emma was certain the girl beside her was going to continue the conversation but she was too caught up in her own thoughts to find the energy to chat to a complete stranger. She turned back to look out of the window as the noise of the plane's engines changed. She searched for signs of life beneath the wings in the red dirt.

Where was the town? The pilot was obviously planning to land somewhere but as far as she could tell only miles and miles of nothing lay beyond the windows. When she'd visited Australia before she'd never travelled away from the coast and the landscape beyond the plane window looked so alien.

The country wasn't completely flat. She could see undulations in the earth, but from this height she only got a sense of their size from the shadows they cast onto the red dirt. There wasn't a speck of green to be seen—even the trees and bushes looked faded and grey. They'd long since left the ocean and the mountains west of Sydney behind and the world she was entering now looked untamed and hostile.

The land was vast and barren and it looked as though it could swallow people. It was no stretch of the imagination to think of people disappearing out here in the back of beyond, never to be seen again. Was she going to survive this?

A sudden wave of homesickness swept through her and the feeling took her by surprise. Although she'd been born and bred in England she'd always longed to really experience the Australian way of life. After all, she was half-Australian, and this was her chance to really immerse herself in the culture, her chance to experience life here as an adult as opposed to the self-absorbed teenager she'd been when she'd last visited.

As a teenager she'd existed on a diet of Australian television, everything from suburban settings to beachside settings to the Outback, but now it seemed that fantasising about the Australian Outback was one thing; actually experiencing it might be something else entirely.

She hoped this trip would give her a chance to heal, a chance to recover from what had been a terrible twelve months and a chance to work out what made her happy, but looking at this foreign landscape she was beginning to think that she might not find the answers here at all. It might take all her strength just to survive. She hoped coming here wasn't going to turn out to be a mistake.

The plane continued to drop lower in the sky and Emma felt the undercarriage of the plane open as the pilot prepared to lower the wheels, but a minute later the plane was levelling out and she heard the flaps close again. She looked out of the window at the red dirt and the greenish-grey, almost leafless trees and stunted bushes. They weren't getting any closer.

The plane's undercarriage opened a second time, before closing again just as rapidly. Emma frowned and watched as the plane began to circle. As the plane turned she could see the airport buildings below them. At least she knew now that there was civilisation out here. That was comforting. But the next words she heard, however, were not.

'Ladies and gentlemen...' The pilot's voice came through the plane's audio system. 'Due to an unforeseen technical problem with the landing gear, I would like to inform you that we will be carrying out an emergency landing.' He paused momentarily and there was complete silence in the plane as every passenger waited to hear what he had to say next.

'However, there is no need to be alarmed. Please remain in your seats with your seat belts tightly fastened. Your cabin crew will pass through the cabin, demonstrating the brace position and landing procedures.'

His tone suggested this was more of an inconvenience than a problem but Emma did wonder how he intended to land the plane. She could only assume he'd been trained for this sort of thing. In her experience pilots were trained for all sorts of emergencies but the pilots she knew flew for the air force, and she had no idea what experience pilots in Outback Australia had. Surely they'd have to return to Sydney? But even as she waited for the pilot to make that announcement she realised it was ridiculous.

Returning to Sydney wouldn't miraculously resolve the problem. The landing gear would still be stuck. It couldn't be fixed in mid-air. So what was he going to do? They couldn't fly around indefinitely. At some stage they'd run out of fuel and then they'd drop out of the sky.

As her fellow passengers also put two and two together

she could feel fear building up around her. Like a living breathing presence in the air it moved from one person to the next, wrapping its icy tentacles around each and every one of them, binding them together in a potential tragedy.

Everyone was silent. Were they thinking about crashing or were they too terrified to utter a sound? Whatever the reason for the silence it was there and it was complete and there was nothing to distract anyone from the pilot's next words.

'This is going to make landing difficult but not impossible. The airport has a dirt landing strip, which we can use in this situation, but I ask you all to assume the crash position as directed by our cabin crew.'

His last sentence succeeded in breaking the silence. There was yelling, there were tears and there was screaming. It seemed as though everyone had found their voices at once and the cabin reverberated with noise. Emma's heart leapt in her chest and she felt it seem to lodge at the base of her throat. Nausea filled the empty space in her ribcage where moments before her heart had been.

In the commotion the crew moved calmly through the cabin. They opened the window shades and instructed the passengers to put their heads into their laps or brace themselves on the seat in front of them. Surely they couldn't be as calm as they sounded?

But gradually, as the plane continued to circle, the cabin crew managed to quieten the passengers and the noise was reduced to a less frightening level.

Emma put her head in her lap. She knew the plane was circling in order to give the emergency crews on the ground time to get into position. She could picture the fire engines and ambulances racing to the edge of the runway and she wondered whose services would be required most.

This was crazy, she thought as she hugged her knees.

She'd flown halfway around the world searching for peace but she hadn't expected it to come in the form of mortality. This was why she should never make plans. They always went wrong. She was going to die at twenty-seven years of age. Just like her mother had.

No. Thinking like that wasn't helpful. She had to believe that the pilot was as confident as he sounded. She took a deep breath and crossed her fingers as the overhead lights were switched off and the cabin was plunged into semi-darkness. The afternoon light bouncing off the desert and coming through the windows was only just bright enough to take the edge off the gloom.

Emma closed her eyes and waited for the moment that everyone talked about. She wasn't waiting for her life to flash before her eyes but for the moment of regret for things she hadn't yet done. But it wasn't things left undone that sprang to mind. It was things she'd lost. Her mother had died when Emma had been a toddler and she barely remembered her, but her father had died recently and Emma felt his loss keenly. She and her father had shared a close bond. For many years it had been just the two of them, and she wished more than anything that he was still part of her life.

She'd tried to fill the void left by her father's death with other relationships but her choice of Jeremy, her last boyfriend, had been disastrous costing her both a place to live and her job.

That was something else she missed, she realised. Her job as a nurse, which she loved. But maybe it was time to put that behind her. Jeremy had said and done some cruel things that had made her question her nursing skills but she shouldn't let him dictate her path. Not any more. She wasn't about to ask for her old job back, she knew she'd never want to work with Jeremy again, but that didn't prevent her from nursing altogether. There were plenty of other hospitals that would love to have her.

Her career was something worth living for and she promised herself that if she survived this landing she would set about returning to nursing.

She had just started running through a mental list of which hospitals she should apply to when her head bounced and her chin slammed against her knees, jarring her teeth as the plane hit the ground and slid on its belly. The collision with the earth took her by surprise as she hadn't realised they were that close.

She could hear the screech of metal as the fuselage complained about being thrown at the ground and she waited for the sound of metal tearing as the plane was ripped apart, waited for the smell of fuel, the roaring heat of flames.

Around her people were screaming, including the girl beside her. Emma opened her eyes. The girl was cradling her left arm and her hand was twisted and lying at an unnatural angle relative to her forearm. She couldn't have been in the brace position properly and she must have slammed into the back of the seat in front of her on impact and fractured her wrist. The break looked painful and, considering their circumstances, there was every chance she'd go into shock. But what could Emma do?

She could feel the plane sliding sideways before it came to a halt. She looked along the aisle. Some of the overhead lockers had sprung open with the impact and contents had fallen out, but incredibly the plane appeared to be in one piece. There were no explosions, no gaping holes, no fires. People were crying but she couldn't see any movement, not from either the crew or the passengers. There was no one to assist them, not yet. What could she do?

Over the sound of crying passengers Emma could hear

the sirens of the emergency vehicles. She looked out the window but the view was completely obscured by a curtain of red dust that billowed around them. The red haze swirled as the emergency vehicles raced through it and the cloud pulsed as the emergency lights bounced off the dust particles. Help was on the way but she couldn't tell how long it would be before they'd be reached.

The girl had stopped screaming but was still cradling her left arm protectively and sobbing. Emma touched the girl lightly on the shoulder, needing to get her attention. 'I think you've broken your wrist,' she said, stating the obvious. 'I'm a nurse. Do you want me to help you?'

The girl looked at Emma. Her face was pale, completely drained of colour, and her eyes were wide. 'I'm a nurse too,' she said, 'but I can't think of what to do.'

Emma understood exactly what the girl meant. Administering treatment to others was vastly different from working out how to self-treat. And even though Emma wasn't used to giving treatment in quite this situation— state-of-the-art emergency departments were more her scene—she knew that any assistance she could give would be beneficial.

She dragged her handbag from under her seat. She knew she probably wasn't supposed to remove it but she needed to do something while they waited. Rummaging through it, she found a packet of painkillers but left them alone. The paramedics would want to be in charge of that.

She dug deeper into her bag and found a large cotton scarf that she carried in case the air-conditioning on the plane was too cold. She gave a wry smile as she pulled it out. Efficient air-conditioning was the least of their problems.

However, she could use the scarf to stabilise the girl's arm because somehow they still had to get out of the plane.

Emma assumed they'd have to exit through the emergency doors, which would mean sliding down the inflatable chutes. That wasn't going to be good. But if she could make the girl more comfortable it might help.

'Would you like me to support your arm with this?' Emma asked, showing her the scarf.

She received a nod and she quickly fashioned a sling, holding the arm close against the girl's body. By the time she'd finished, the cabin crew had got the emergency exits open and were moving through the aircraft, organising the evacuation process. Any injured passengers and those travelling with young children were directed to evacuate first.

A flight attendant stopped by the girl's side. Emma wasn't sure if she'd noticed the sling or just the girl's pallor. She addressed them both. 'Are you travelling together?'

'No,' Emma answered. 'But she's broken her wrist and she needs medical attention.'

'Are you injured?' the flight attendant asked Emma, and when Emma shook her head she continued with another question. 'Can you get off the plane with her? We prefer not to evacuate injured passengers alone and we're all needed up here.'

Emma nodded. She unclipped her seat belt and slung her bag across her chest. She stood up behind the girl and they joined the queue of passengers waiting to be evacuated. Emma slid her sandals from her feet and took the girl's flip-flops and held both pairs of shoes in one hand.

The flight attendant instructed the girl to evacuate first, with Emma following. She paused at the top of the slide as the heat took her breath away. It was oppressive, dry and intense, a bit like standing in front of a furnace. The air burnt her lungs as she breathed it but while it was dusty she couldn't smell fuel or fire. The heat wasn't coming from flames but rising from the red desert sand.

Aware of others queuing behind her, she hurriedly sat at the top of the chute and slid to the ground. She got to her feet on shaky legs and went to the girl with the broken wrist, who was looking dazed and bewildered. She led her away from the chute, away from the streams of people pouring out of the crippled plane, and sat her down.

'Sit here, I'll go and look for help,' she told her as she helped her to the ground. She dropped their shoes beside her and left her sitting in the shade of the plane as she set off in search of the ambulances.

By now there were people everywhere, passengers, airline crew, airport staff and emergency workers, and the chaotic surroundings were exacerbated by the dusty conditions, which made it difficult to see who was who.

A shape materialised out of the red haze in front of her and transformed into a tall, long-legged man with a strong, muscular frame. A rather attractive, rugged man in uniform. For a moment she thought her mind was playing tricks on her, that perhaps she *had* bumped her head. But then he spoke to her.

'Are you all right? Have you been separated from someone?'

He was real. His voice was deep, undoubtedly Australian, but his tone was relaxed and somewhat calming against the noisy background.

Emma shook her head.

'Are you injured?'

Emma shook her head again. She felt perfectly fine. Possibly a bit disoriented but physically okay.

He was staring at her. So she stared back.

CHAPTER TWO

She had to look up to see him properly. He was tall, at a guess she'd say five inches taller than her, which would make him about six feet three. His eyes were a clear blue, quite striking against his tanned skin, and his hair was thick and dark with a slight curl. His shoulders were broad and he was solidly built but it appeared to be all muscle. He looked like he could muster sheep or cattle, or whatever it was they farmed out here, all day, and still have energy to spare.

She almost sighed with pleasure. Her first glimpse of an Outback man and he was just what she'd imagined, just what her hours of watching Australian television dramas had led her to hope for. He was gorgeous in a ruggedly handsome way.

While she was busy drooling over his gorgeousness she realised he was still staring at her, waiting for her to answer. He probably thought she was in shock.

'I'm fine,' she replied.

'You've got blood on your lip,' he said.

Despite the noise and disorder surrounding them, Emma didn't need to strain to hear his words. His deep voice carried easily across the small distance that separated them. He was holding a small first-aid backpack and he took some tissues from it and held them out to her.

Emma licked her lip and tasted blood, warm and salty, on her tongue. She must have bitten it when the plane had belly-flopped onto the landing strip. As she took the tissue and pressed it to her lip she was surprised to find that her hand was shaking. Adrenalin was coursing through her system but she hadn't had time to notice until now.

'You've missed a bit,' he said when Emma took the tissue from her lip. He delved into the backpack again and retrieved a bottle of water. He poured a little on the tissues. 'May I?' he asked.

His clear blue eyes were fixed on hers, drawing her in, relaxing her. The chaos, the noise and the crowd of people around them seemed to disappear into the red dust, leaving the two of them alone on the airstrip. The experience was slightly hypnotic and Emma found herself nodding automatically in reaction to his calming blue gaze.

But when he reached out and cupped her chin with his hand her response was definitely not calm and relaxed, it was something completely different altogether. Her skin tingled under his touch as his fingertips grazed her lip, leaving a trail of heat behind as he wiped the blood from her face.

She couldn't speak, she couldn't move, she could barely breathe. Her breaths were shallow but it was the best she could manage, and she could feel her heart pulsing in her chest. She told herself it wasn't him, it was the adrenalin that had heightened her senses. What other possible reason could there be? She didn't have this kind of reaction to perfect strangers. No one did. Did they?

She needed to sit down and catch her breath. She needed to get some perspective. She just needed a moment to collect herself and then everything would be back to normal. She couldn't afford to get spellbound by tall, dark and handsome men. By any men. Not right now.

'Do you want someone to look at that?' he asked.

His question confused her. He was wearing a blue short-sleeved shirt with epaulettes on the shoulders and on his breast pocket was a logo she recognised, a pair of wings, the symbol of the flying doctors service. Why would he get someone else to look at her lip?

'What do you mean?' she asked, aware that her voice was shaky and thin. She sounded as out of breath as she felt.

'Did you want me to get one of the medics to check it for you?' he asked.

Emma glanced at the logo on his shirt pocket again before she looked up at him. 'Aren't you a doctor?'

He shook his head. 'I'm a pilot.'

'Oh.'

A pilot. His answer threw her off course for a moment. She hadn't expected that.

'I'll be okay,' she said. She was a nurse with a bloody lip, she was sure she didn't need to take up anybody's time for that. And then she remembered what she'd been doing before she'd been distracted by the appearance of a handsome pilot in her path. 'But there's a girl back here with a broken wrist, I was looking for a paramedic.'

'Can you take me to her?'

She nodded. 'It's this way.'

She retraced her steps and he fell into step beside her.

She watched the ground to make sure she didn't tread on anything dangerous. She couldn't believe she hadn't thought to put her sandals back on her feet, but it also kept her attention focussed on the job at hand. She'd never realised she could be so easily distracted.

Within moments they were back in the shadow of the plane and the handsome stranger picked up his pace and ran the remaining few steps.

'Lisa! What happened?'

'Harry!'

Emma heard the happiness in the girl's voice even as she registered that her name was Lisa. Lisa and Harry. Lisa knew Harry. Harry knew Lisa. They knew each other.

Good, Emma told herself. This handsome stranger was nothing to her. It was just the adrenalin that had caused such an unexpected physical reaction, just the adrenalin that had left her short of breath and made her skin tingle. She could ignore the little flutter of excitement in her belly, the little increase in her heart rate. Even if she'd been in the market for a man, and she wasn't, it looked like this one was well and truly off limits.

'I got caught in the wrong position. I wasn't braced properly,' Lisa replied. 'It was stupid of me.'

'Let's get you to an ambulance,' Harry was saying, and before Emma could blink he'd crouched down and scooped Lisa into his arms. He stood up again, lifting her as if she weighed no more than a three-year-old.

'Thank you for your help.' He was holding Lisa in his arms but he was talking to her. Emma was surprised—she hadn't expected him to remember she was there. 'Do you think you can follow the others to the terminal?' he asked as he inclined his head to his left.

Emma wondered if she shouldn't offer to help other passengers. Surely any help would be gratefully received but as she looked around, now that the dust had settled, she could see paramedics attending to those who needed them and there was a line of uninjured passengers making their way across the dirt towards a small building. Things looked to be under control.

She nodded. She was fine. She could walk. She just needed to put her shoes back on. Her sandals were still lying on the ground and as she bent to retrieve them she caught sight of her filthy clothes. In the few minutes that she'd been out of the plane she'd become covered in a layer of red dust. She slid her dusty feet into her sandals and glanced back up at the man standing before her. His clothes were immaculate, clean and crisp and she wondered how he had managed to stay so pristine.

'Yes, I can,' she answered as she deliberately straightened her shoulders. She was okay. She could manage. 'I'm fine. Go, get Lisa to the ambulance. I'm fine,' she repeated, aware that she didn't need to monopolise any more of his time.

Emma turned and walked away so that he was free to leave. She followed the crowd towards the terminal and left the gorgeous stranger behind in the red dust, making herself look straight ahead even though she wanted to turn around for another glimpse. No doubt he was already whisking Lisa off to the paramedics and would have no time to give her another thought. She wondered if she'd wake up tomorrow and think this was all a dream. Or if she'd run into him again.

As she entered the little terminal building she couldn't resist a final glance over her shoulder but he was nowhere to be seen, already absorbed into the throng that remained gathered around the stricken aircraft.

Inside the terminal a representative from the airline was issuing instructions, handing out paperwork and getting details on whether passengers wanted to wait for their luggage or have it delivered. Emma was swept up in a sea of red tape and it was many minutes before she had a chance to wonder where Sophie was.

She searched the area for a familiar face but she couldn't spot her cousin anywhere. She frowned. With all the drama of the crash landing she would have thought Sophie would be front and centre, waiting to welcome her. Was she in the right place? Was there more than one back of beyond in Outback Australia? God, imagine if she'd crash-landed in the wrong town!

She pulled her mobile phone out of her handbag and switched it on. She was almost certain she was in the right place. There was bound to be a reason Soph wasn't here. Perhaps she'd left a message.

Sure enough, her phone beeped as soon as it came to life.

So sorry, Em, clinic running late, will be there by six. S xx

Emma shrugged her slim shoulders and sat down to wait. There was nothing else for her to do. She watched the other travellers coming and going, their numbers dwindling as the terminal building emptied out. Everyone else seemed to have someone to meet them or somewhere to go. The ambulances had long since departed and Emma wondered how Lisa was and what had happened to the pilot.

She watched as the fire engines drove away from the scene, leaving the plane stranded in the middle of nowhere. She knew how it felt. She wondered how the plane would be moved and assumed it would be towed somewhere, somehow. It was sitting abandoned. Had the luggage been retrieved? What had happened to her bag?

She frowned and started searching for a baggage carousel even as she realised she hadn't seen one. She should go and fetch her bag. She stood up. She would need to make some enquiries.

The first person she saw was the ruggedly handsome pilot. Harry, Lisa had called him. He was walking towards her. He walked quickly, his long strides eating up the distance between them, and she expected him to continue on past her as he looked as though he was walking with a purpose, but he came to stop in front of her.

'Are you still here? Is someone meeting you?' He assessed her with his blue gaze as his eyebrows came together in a frown.

Emma looked up at him. He towered over her, but his size wasn't intimidating, in fact she found it oddly reassuring. He gave off a sense that he was a man who could be relied on, a man who would get things done. Maybe it was just the uniform, she'd always seen uniforms as a symbol of order and control, but she sensed that with this man it was more about his personality and less about his attire.

'Yes, but they're running late,' she replied. 'I'm just going to look for my bags while I wait. Do you know where the baggage carousel is?'

'First time in Broken Hill?' he asked.

He was smiling and by the expression in his bright blue eyes she could tell he wanted to laugh. At her. She couldn't imagine what there was to laugh about but whatever it was that amused him he at least had the good grace not to laugh out loud.

'Yes, why?'

Harry watched as Emma straightened her slim shoulders and lifted her chin and he knew she was just daring him to make fun of her. He wasn't about to take the mickey out of her, not when she'd just had a less than stellar welcome to the Hill, but he always found it amusing to see how first-timers coped with Broken Hill. Listening to her English accent, he imagined that in her case it would be a vastly different experience from anything she'd had before. He wondered what she was doing here, this English girl in the middle of the Outback. She didn't look like the average backpacker and she appeared to be travelling alone. What could possibly have brought her here? Who was she waiting for?

'There is no carousel,' he explained. 'Your luggage will be outside on the trolley. It's this way.' He could have directed her to the trolley, it wasn't difficult to find if you knew where to look, but he wasn't in a hurry and he'd never been able to resist a damsel in distress, especially not a pretty one.

He'd seen her again the moment he'd entered the terminal and he'd kept one eye on her even as he'd helped get other passengers sorted. Technically, sorting out the chaos from the crash landing wasn't his job but in a town like Broken Hill, where everyone knew everybody else, or at least that's what it felt like, many hands made light work. Particularly in situations like this, when things had gone haywire, it was the country way to pitch in and do your bit. But he'd made sure he'd done his bit while keeping an eye on the tall, willowy brunette.

The terminal was almost empty now. Most of the passengers had been taken care of and only a few remained. She was one of them.

He'd half turned away from her, towards the exit and the baggage trolley, waiting for her to follow him, but she wasn't moving. She was standing still and frowning. A little crease had appeared between her green eyes and she was fiddling with the end of her ponytail.

A moment later she appeared to come to a decision. She flicked her hair back over her shoulder and he watched as she stowed her mobile phone in her handbag. Her wrists were brown and slender, her fingers slim with short, polished nails, and her movements as she slung her bag over her shoulder were fluid and graceful. Even though her white cotton dress and silver sandals were covered in red dust, she still managed to look elegant.

Her outfit alone was enough to convince Harry she wasn't a local. Not too many people were brave enough to wear all white in the country's red centre.

But it wasn't her outfit that had told him she wasn't from around here. Neither was it her English accent. Even before she'd spoken one word or asked the question about her luggage Harry had known she wasn't from the Hill. He knew he'd never seen her before. He would have remembered.

'Did you want to come with me to the trolley?' he asked, eager to prolong the encounter. His offer was rewarded with a smile that made him catch his breath. Her green eyes sparkled but it was the twin dimples that appeared on each side of her mouth that made him do a double take. At first glance there was no denying she was an attractive woman but when she smiled she was spectacular.

She reminded him of the wildflowers that suddenly appeared after the desert rains—stunningly beautiful and completely unexpected—and he wondered if, like the native flowers, she would appear fragile yet turn out to be resilient.

'Thank you,' she said without protest. She didn't tell him she'd be able to find the luggage trolley on her own; she didn't tell him she didn't need his help.

She simply fell into step beside him and made him feel good about himself for helping. He watched the reaction of the remaining passengers as they walked through the terminal. He was used to being with beautiful women but it seemed as though every person in the building was looking at them and he didn't flatter himself that he was the one who'd captured their attention. It was most definitely the willowy brunette they were watching.

He felt like the schoolboy who'd caught the attention of the prom queen. He knew that was ridiculous and fanciful but that made no difference—it was how she made him feel and the sensation was unexpected but not unpleasant.

The half-laden luggage trolley sat just outside the terminal doors.

Emma reached up to grab a large duffel bag from the top of the pile.

'Here, let me get that for you,' he offered. 'It looks heavy.'

She could have managed to lift her bag and find the trolley, she'd just needed to know where it was. But she didn't tell him she could manage because she found him fascinating and she was more than happy to let him help her. So she stepped back to let him past her.

As he retrieved her bag from the trolley his biceps bulged, straining against the fabric of his shirt. She'd bet her last pound that his muscles came from physical work, not from lifting weights in a gym. He looked vibrant, healthy and solid, totally male. He seemed a far more masculine version of the men she was used to in England.

Maybe it was the tougher environment out here, maybe it was the sun, the fresh air or the physical activity, but, whatever it was, someone had definitely got something right when they'd made him.

'You're staying in town for a while?' he asked as he hefted her bag and slung it over his shoulder.

He was grinning and once again she had the feeling that he was doing his best not to laugh at her. She knew her bag was heavy, even though he made it look light.

When she'd packed she hadn't really known what she'd need and as usual she knew she would have brought far too many pairs of shoes. She'd already noticed that everyone in the airport wore no-nonsense sturdy shoes or flip-flops and she hadn't seen one pair of sparkly shoes on anyone over the age of thirteen.

She knew her bag was bulging at the seams and she knew she might not need the three pairs of strappy stilettos she'd packed, or even the two pairs of ballet flats, but surely she didn't have to sacrifice her fashion sense completely just because she was in the middle of nowhere?

'I'm not sure,' she replied. Her plans hadn't evolved at all past getting on the plane and arriving in town.

'What brings you here?' He was frowning as he carried her bag into the terminal.

'I'm visiting my cousin.'

'Is that who's running late?'

She nodded in reply.

'How late?' he asked.

Emma checked her watch and felt his eyes follow her movement. 'About an hour. She sent me a message, something about the clinic running late.'

'The clinic?' he queried. 'What does she do, this cousin of yours?'

'Do you always ask this many questions?' she countered, wondering if it was the country manner to be this direct or just his manner.

'Yep,' he answered, with a smile that made his blue eyes sparkle.

'Sophie's a physio at the hospital,' she told him, realising she'd tell him just about anything he wanted to know provided he was smiling at her.

'You're not talking about Sophie Stewart, are you?'

'Yes, do you know her?'

He was nodding.

Just exactly how small was this town? Emma wondered. First he'd known Lisa and now Sophie. But it was good news for her as it meant she was in the right place after all.

'She's out on a clinic run with the flying doctors,' he

said. 'There's a storm out over Innamincka that's delayed
their return.'

Emma remembered Sophie mentioning something about
the allied health hospital staff sometimes working with the
flying doctor service. Her eyes flicked to the logo on his
shirt pocket, the wings of the flying doctors. Soph got to
work with this man? No wonder she'd said she planned to
stay in Broken Hill for a while.

'I'm a pilot with the flying doctors,' he said when he
saw the direction of her gaze. 'I'm Harry Connor...' he
extended his hand '...and it's a pleasure to meet you, Sophie's cousin.'

'Emma. My name is Emma Matheson,' she replied, as
she reached for his hand.

And there it was again. That same tingle that made her
catch her breath. The feeling that he was taking all her
oxygen and causing her light-headedness. Only this time
she couldn't blame adrenalin. That had had plenty of time
to settle while she'd been sitting waiting.

'So, Emma Matheson, what do you plan to do now?' he
said as he released her hand.

She wasn't big on plans but fortunately Harry hadn't
finished. He continued speaking and gave her some options. 'Did you want to hang around here? Or you could
wait at the flying doctor base or I could drop you off at
Sophie's place.'

'I don't have a key.'

He laughed. Out loud this time and it was such a pleasant sound, deep and full and it resonated through her. It
was so genuine she couldn't find it irritating, even though
she knew it was at her expense. 'I doubt the house is locked
and if it is I know where the key is hidden.'

Did he and Sophie have history? And what about Lisa?
He read her mind. 'Don't look at me like that. It's all

perfectly innocent. And I promise I'm completely trust-worthy.'

She doubted very much that he was innocent but she wanted to believe she could trust him. Jeremy's behaviour had shaken her faith in men but she had a good association with men in uniforms. Besides, she'd seen how he treated Lisa and he knew Sophie. She wanted to think he was a man who could be trusted, and with a laugh like that, one that reached right into his bright blue eyes, how could he be anything but nice?

'Now, where can I take you?' he asked, obviously de-ciding she'd had enough time to make up her mind.

'If it's not too much trouble, I'd love to go to Sophie's. I need a shower and a change of clothes.'

'Done.'

'But aren't you supposed to be working?'

'Nope. My shift's over. I came across to the airport when I heard the distress call. I have clearance to be on the airport apron and I thought I might be needed. Turns out I am.' He grinned and Emma's insides skittered. She wasn't about to complain about his presence. It did feel as though he'd been sent to help her.

'Come with me,' he invited. 'Send Sophie a text and let her know I'll drop you at her place—that way you know I'll have to get you there safely,' he added as Emma still hesitated.

'That's not...' Emma was about to protest and say it wasn't that she didn't trust him but she knew that was ex-actly the issue. And Harry knew it too. She nodded—it was a good suggestion. She pulled her phone out and sent Sophie a message even as she decided to consider this one of those times when things were going to unfold without her input. A pilot, in uniform, who'd already helped her and Lisa. If she was going to learn to put her faith in people again, this was as good a place as any to start.

Harry waited for her to put her phone away before he headed for the exit. Emma had to hurry to keep up with his long strides as he walked through the terminal. Not even the weight of her bag, which he still had slung over his shoulder like a beach towel, slowed him down. Not that his strength should have surprised her considering how easily he'd lifted Lisa earlier.

Harry loaded her bag into the boot of a large four-wheel drive and held the passenger door open for her. As they left the airport he pointed out the sights as he drove across town.

Normally Emma would have debated whether what he was showing her qualified as 'sights' as in her opinion the best thing she could see was Harry and she was more than happy to keep him in her view. But she didn't want to appear rude so she tried to look interested as he showed her another sight—a huge pile of dirt in the centre of town.

According to him, this was the old mine and the reason for Broken Hill's existence. The town had been founded on the back of a mining boom when lead, zinc and silver had been found in the area, but Emma found it hard to get excited about a heap of dirt, although she did agree that it made a useful landmark.

Emma tried to remember what Sophie had told her about the town as Harry negotiated the streets. She knew it was first and foremost a mining town but there was also a thriving artists' community and it was a popular location for movie-making. Looking around, Emma couldn't imagine why but apparently the surrounding country was quite spectacular. Sophie had told her there wasn't enough in the town itself to keep her occupied for the three months she planned to stay, which was why she'd spent the first month in Sydney with the rest of Sophie's family. Soph had popped back for a weekend, which had given them time to catch up, but Emma was looking forward to spending more time with her cousin. Sophie was always like a breath of fresh air and Emma needed that.

Sophie's house was on one side of the mine and the airport was on the other, but even so it took less than twenty minutes to arrive at the house. It was a large, old, single-level, double-fronted stone building with a wide veranda and iron roof, and Emma remembered that Sophie shared the house. It was much too big for one person.

'Sophie shares with a girl called Grace, is that right?' Emma asked, as she followed Harry along the driveway. She'd expected him to try the front door but instead he was walking down the side of the house and entering through the back. Just as he'd predicted, the door was unlocked.

'Yes, she's a flying doctor,' Harry replied, as he led Emma through a casual living room and up the hall. 'She was on the clinic run today with Sophie. This is their spare room,' he said, as he opened a bedroom door and deposited her bag. 'If you're okay, I might call past the hospital and check on Lisa. Will you be all right here on your own?'

Lucky Lisa. Emma nodded. 'I'll be fine. I'll have a shower and a cup of tea. Thanks for the lift.'

'No worries.' Harry's responses were as easygoing as he appeared to be, and Emma was sorry to see him go. She was suddenly aware of how big and empty and quiet the house was now that she was alone so she headed for the bathroom and the comfort of a hot shower, wanting to keep busy until Sophie got home.

She had showered and changed into shorts and a strappy tank top and was sitting at the kitchen table with a pot of tea in front of her when Sophie exploded in through the back door. There was no other way to describe it, Soph only ever seemed to have one pace and that was full steam ahead.

'You made it! I can't believe you're actually here,' she squealed. 'I heard about the plane trip. Thank God it didn't crash.'

Emma didn't know what else you'd call it when a plane dropped from the sky and slid along a runway on its belly instead of its wheels, but she agreed it could have been worse, much worse, so she wasn't about to argue.

'I'm so sorry I was late. Are you really okay?' Sophie looked her up and down.

'I'm fine.'

'You've got a bit of a fat lip.'

Emma touched her lip self-consciously. It was tender but it was hardly a catastrophe. She started to stand but Sophie had enveloped her in a hug before she could get out of her seat. 'I'm fine, really. All in one piece and delivered safe and sound to your door.'

'I can't believe you've met Harry already. How did he know who you were?'

'He didn't at first. He was on the landing strip when we were all evacuated from the plane. He sort of appeared from nowhere through the dust—'

'Did you collapse into his arms and make him carry you to the terminal?'

Emma shot her cousin a withering glare. 'No.'

'Pity,' Sophie said with an exaggerated sigh. 'That would have been so romantic.'

Emma ignored that comment. She happened to agree with Sophie but it would have sounded ridiculous to say so. 'He had his arms full already.'

'With what?' Sophie asked.

'With a nurse called Lisa,' Emma said, keen to see Sophie's reaction to that bit of news.

'A short, curvaceous, blonde?'

Emma nodded, unsurprised that Sophie knew her. She was fast realising that anonymity was hard to find in this town.

'What happened to her?'

'She broke her wrist. Harry carried her off to the ambulance. He asked if I was okay and sent me to the terminal by myself.' Emma left out the part about the tingles and the light-headedness as in her opinion it was far better to play down the events of the afternoon. 'But when I was waiting for you, and the terminal was just about empty, he came and helped me again.'

'I still think it would have been better if he'd swept *you* off your feet instead of Lisa but never mind—isn't he fabulous?'

Gorgeous, Emma thought, but she wasn't going to say that until she had more information. She knew from experience that things were not always as they seemed. 'He seems nice.'

'Nice! He's better than that. If I wasn't madly in love with Mark, I'd chase after him.'

'He's single?' That surprised her. In her experience men who looked like that weren't often single. 'What about Lisa?'

'They're just friends. Harry's single but he's never single for long. He has a bit of a reputation as a ladies' man. Luckily for him, Broken Hill is a very transient place, which means lots of the women with broken hearts are just passing through and don't stay around to cause him grief. It seems to suit Harry. I'm sure his motto is "plenty more fish in the sea". I bet he'd be happy to help you get over Jeremy.'

'I don't need help. Distance is all I need. I think I'm done with dating for a while.'

'We'll see.' Sophie laughed.

'What's that supposed to mean?'

'I've never known you to be without a boyfriend for more than a few months and it's been, what? Four months now?'

'Five.' Not that she was counting. But Sophie was right. She was never single for long and didn't actually like being on her own. She'd spent too much time on her own as a child and because of her nomadic upbringing she'd never really had a chance to form close female friendships that stood the test of time so boyfriends had filled that gap. But Emma did intend to take a break from dating.

She needed time to find out who she was and what she wanted, without any complications. 'I'm not looking for a boyfriend.'

'That's okay,' Sophie said, refusing to be put off. 'I doubt Harry's looking for a girlfriend but if you have an itch that needs scratching, he'd probably be happy to help you out.'

'I'll keep that in mind,' Emma replied, even though she knew she had no intention of getting romantically involved with anyone for a long time, no matter how gorgeous they were.

Not even if his touch had sent her hormones into overdrive?

Surely that was only because it had been so long since she'd had sex. Five months was a very long time so was it any wonder her hormones were a little crazy? But before Sophie could make any more helpful suggestions, their discussion was interrupted by the arrival of Sophie's housemate.

Grace was a petite woman, short and fine boned with jet-black hair cut in a bob. She was almost the perfect opposite of tall, blonde, Nordic-looking Sophie, and seeing them standing side by side as Sophie introduced her made Emma smile.

Grace's arrival was closely followed by Harry's reappearance and as he let himself in through the back door and despite her vows of celibacy, Emma found herself wishing she'd changed into a slightly more attractive outfit. She had an enormous bag stuffed with pretty clothes and she'd gone for comfort over style. But at least her hair was freshly washed and blow-dried and she was no longer covered in red dust.

Not that Harry even seemed to notice, he was too busy regaling Grace with his version of the drama of the plane crash while Sophie played hostess. Somehow Harry managed to make the plane crash sound almost exciting and if Emma hadn't been intimately acquainted with the events of the day she would certainly now feel as though she'd lived through it. He was an entertaining storyteller and Emma imagined that anyone listening to his version would be sorry they hadn't seen it for themselves, Harry made it sound as though it had been something not to be missed.

Grace asked Emma a few questions and Emma added her comments as best she could, but she was no match for Harry's engaging style and she preferred listening to him while they waited for delivery of the take-away pizza Sophie had ordered.

'Lisa's broken wrist is a complication we don't need at the moment,' Harry said as he munched his fourth piece of pizza. Emma wasn't surprised that a man of his size had a hearty appetite.

'Why is that?' Sophie asked.

'She's supposed to be taking a locum position with the flying doctor service while Kerri is on maternity leave. She was due to start next week but she'll be out of action now.'

'Why don't you do it, Em?' Sophie said. 'Emma's a nurse,' she added for Harry and Grace's benefit.

'A hospital nurse,' Emma clarified.

'You're trained in emergency work, though,' Sophie added.

'Are you?' Grace asked, and when Emma nodded her face lit up. 'Do you think you'd be interested?'

'What, in working with the flying doctor service?'

'Yes,' Grace replied.

'I'm here on a tourist visa. I'm not allowed to work,' Emma said, thinking that surely Grace's comment was just one of those off-the-cuff remarks people made without any real intent behind it.

'I think you can do volunteer work,' Grace said.

Emma shrugged. 'I'm not sure I'm qualified to work with the flying doctors.'

'If you've got emergency training, you'll be fine.'

'Yes, but I'm trained to work in a hospital, not out in a field in the middle of nowhere,' she protested. She didn't know the first thing about nursing outside a hospital environment and she hadn't even done that for four months. Grace must be mad to think it was something she could do.

'Technically it won't be a field.' Sophie laughed. 'Out here we call them paddocks and the chances are you'll just be in the dirt in the middle of nowhere, but it's a once-in-a-lifetime experience. You couldn't get enough of that flying doctors show when we were teenagers; imagine getting to do the real thing.'

'I'm sure it's hardly the same.' She had loved that television series but to hear Sophie say it, in front of people who actually did it for a living, made her sound like a crazy groupie.

But Sophie wasn't going to give up. 'Are you kidding? It's brilliant! I reckon you'd love it.'

Harry caught Emma's eye. He was grinning at her and suddenly the proposition seemed quite appealing. Maybe it would be fun.

'You don't need to decide today. You've probably had enough to deal with,' he said, coming to her rescue once again. 'But why don't you come out to the base and have a look around? You can't judge the job on an ancient television drama.'

'That's true,' Grace added. 'We work harder and we're not all as good looking.'

'Don't scare her off, Grace,' Harry said, laughing, and Emma relaxed. That was a sound she could get used to.

'At least go and have a look, Em,' Sophie encouraged her. 'It's not like you've got any other plans. You said you thought you'd stay for a while.'

Emma nodded. Soph was right, she wasn't in a hurry to go home. There wasn't anything to hurry back for. Her family was there, what was left of it, but they'd still be there whenever she returned. She'd left her job and she didn't have another one waiting. She definitely wasn't planning on going back to her old job, there were too many people there who knew her business. She was here for two more months and she didn't intend to go back to London before that, which meant she really did need to come up with another option. And hadn't she promised herself that if she survived the crash landing she'd look at returning to nursing?

'You might as well have something to keep you busy.' Sophie's words echoed Emma's thoughts.

'It could be the perfect solution,' Grace added. 'Why don't I get Irene to check out the volunteer situation? I'm sure there's a loophole there somewhere.'

'And in the meantime you could drive out to the base tomorrow to have a look. You'll show her around, won't you, Harry?' Sophie sounded innocent enough but Emma recognised the gleam in her eye.

She chose to pretend not to notice. It seemed as if her life was being organised for her, at least for the next few weeks, but as she had no firm plans of her own there was nothing to argue about.

'I'll think about it,' she said. After all, what harm could there be in just looking?

CHAPTER THREE

BUT she didn't think about it any further until the next morning. She slept well, despite the events of the previous day, and when she woke the sun was already high in the cloudless, blue sky.

Sophie had left a note saying she'd walked to the hospital for her eight o'clock start but she'd left her car keys so Emma could drive out to the flying doctor base.

Did she really want to do that?

It couldn't hurt to go and have a look, could it? It would be interesting to see the base and it didn't mean she had to apply for a job. She wasn't sure what she wanted to do. But when did she ever know? When had she ever had a plan? She'd tried a couple of times but her plans had a habit of going distinctly pear-shaped. Perhaps she was better off sticking to her usual style, which was pretty random.

She had a shower, made herself some toast, did the dishes, watered some of Sophie's plants that looked rather thirsty and when she ran out of things to do she switched on Sophie's computer, logged in to her emails and printed off a copy of her CV, which she'd stored online. Telling herself it didn't hurt to take it with her just in case, it didn't mean she wanted the job, she picked up the car keys and the map Sophie had left for her and headed out the door.

The drive across town—coming from London she

couldn't bring herself to think of Broken Hill as a city—along the almost deserted, dusty streets took the same amount of time as yesterday—not quite twenty minutes. Which was not enough time to work out what she intended to do once she got to the flying doctor base. She sat in Sophie's car for another ten minutes until she realised she couldn't remain there for the rest of the morning.

Viewed from the car park, the flying doctors building was modern and much larger than she'd expected. She walked through a pleasant grassed courtyard, pushed open the door and stepped into the cool, dark foyer. A sign in front of her directed her to head left for the museum or right for the shop and tours.

She hesitated, thinking the museum might be worth a look, but she knew that was just further procrastination. Harry had offered to show her around and if she could have him as her tour guide around the real-life base she didn't need to look at the museum. She hoped he would be there and not off flying the plane somewhere. There was only one way to find out.

Emma stepped to the right and introduced herself to the lady behind the counter.

'Harry told us to expect you. Can you wait here for just a second and I'll fetch Irene,' the woman said, before she disappeared through a swing door that was set into the wall behind her, leaving Emma staring after her.

The woman returned within a minute, followed by a short, round woman who was speaking to Emma before she'd even come through the door.

'Emma, hello, I'm Irene, the base manager. It's good to meet you.' She reached out and grabbed Emma's hand as she was talking and shook it vigorously. 'Why don't you come through to my office and we can talk about the job? I can't believe our luck that you're here and able to work.'

Emma tried to protest as she trailed behind Irene down a short flight of stairs and along a corridor. 'I'm not sure that I can work,' she said. She also wasn't sure if she wanted to.

'You can work on a volunteer basis,' Irene told her. 'Grace was right about that. So if you're interested in a volunteer position, I'm sure we can work something out. Besides, if you're in town for a while you'll soon realise there's not a lot to keep you occupied. You'll soon get bored so you might as well work. Think of it as good experience.'

Emma could tell that Irene wasn't a person who could easily be dissuaded once her mind was made up. This town seemed to be full of strong-willed people. She'd need to try a different tack or she knew she'd find herself signed up before the day was over.

'I might not have the qualifications you're after. I've never worked outside a hospital before.'

But Irene was not going to be put off. 'Neither have most of our nurses when they first come to us. I was told you've got Emergency experience, is that right?'

Emma nodded as Irene led her into an office and closed the door. The office had one glass wall that overlooked a larger, open-plan office that appeared to be a communications centre. The walls were covered with whiteboards, charts and maps and there were several staff members at work within the room.

'If you have emergency experience, I'm sure we'll want you,' Irene said as she indicated to Emma to take a seat. 'Did you bring your CV?'

Emma was in shock. She had her CV in her bag but she hadn't really expected to hand it over. She'd expected to have a relaxed tour of the facility with Harry! Nevertheless, she dug her CV out of her bag and handed it to Irene.

'We're desperate for nurses,' Irene explained. 'We're already down one. Mary's gone to Adelaide to look after her mum who's undergoing chemo, and with Kerri about to go on maternity leave and Lisa with her broken arm, we're going to be short two nurses. One we can cover, two is impossible. I've looked into the volunteering situation and that's perfectly acceptable with the board so as long as your references and qualifications are okay. If that all pans out, you can consider the locum position yours.'

Emma didn't know whether she should be flattered or terrified. She had no idea what she was getting herself into.

Irene leant back in her chair. 'Now, I suppose I should let you ask me some questions. What do you want to know?'

Anything and everything, Emma thought. She had no idea how the flying doctor service actually worked or what they did other than what she'd seen on television, and from what Harry had told her last night it sounded as though the show might have been more fiction than fact.

Before she could work out which question to begin with she heard the sound of a door opening behind her and a familiar voice broke the silence.

'Emma! I heard you were here. How are you? Have you recovered from yesterday?'

Harry.

Emma turned at the sound of his voice. It was just as deep and soothing as she remembered. It reverberated through her and despite the fact that Irene was sitting a few inches away Harry's voice made her feel as if she was the only person he could see.

'Yes, thanks, I'm good. A bit shell-shocked but that has nothing to do with yesterday.'

Harry laughed. 'Irene has that effect on people. Has she convinced you to join us yet? She doesn't like to take no for an answer.'

'I got that impression,' she replied.

Luckily Irene didn't seem to take offence at being discussed like this. 'Harry, do you think you could give Emma the grand tour?' she asked. 'Use your persuasive charms on her to sell the position?'

'That's why I'm here,' Harry answered.

'Good,' Irene replied, and turned back to Emma. 'You could go out on a clinic run tomorrow if you like. Why don't you let me know what you think when you've finished with Harry?' Irene stood and ushered Emma and Harry out the door.

Emma followed Harry through the communications centre and out into another long, narrow corridor. His broad shoulders almost touched the walls on each side, making the corridor seem narrower than it probably was. Harry was the sort of man who needed to be outdoors, Emma thought. She could imagine him on horseback, galloping across the red dirt in jeans and one of those wide-brimmed bushman's hats. She could just imagine how easy it would be to be swept away by the romance of the scene and ride off into the sunset on the back of Harry's horse. She shook her head; her imagination was starting to sound like Sophie.

Still, his ruggedness was better suited to the open air, she thought as she tried to picture him in the cockpit of a small plane. She wondered how he'd look there. Probably just as gorgeous but maybe a bit trapped. It was hard to imagine his energy and size contained in a small space.

'Are you sure you're okay?'

Harry had stopped by a door at the end of the corridor, no doubt wondering why she hadn't said anything.

Emma nodded as she quickly thought of an appropriate response. 'Irene's a bit of a whirlwind, isn't she? I had no idea what she was talking about half the time. And what was that clinic run she mentioned? I don't even know what that is.'

'Clinic runs are flights we do out to the rural towns. Our staff run clinics in the outpatient health centres there,' Harry explained. 'It's really the main part of our work. It's not all emergency retrievals that we do but, because that sounds more exciting, it's what everyone tends to associate with the flying doctors. Every day there are flights out to regional centres so that people living in the more remote areas have access to health care. Some of the trips are for a couple of days and there's always a nurse, usually a doctor and often a dentist or physio or maybe a specialist from the city like an ENT. That was what Sophie was doing yesterday. You should come. It'll be fun.'

'You're going?'

'I am tomorrow. It's my job, remember? Flying planes,' he teased.

She remembered. It was just that she still couldn't imagine how he would fit into the cockpit.

'You like the clinic runs?' she asked.

'To be perfectly honest, I prefer the emergency flights. They're a bit more challenging from my point of view, landing on narrow roads, dodging sheep and cattle, flying into unlit landing strips and through thunderstorms.'

'I'm not sure you're selling the job to me. One botched landing is enough for me for this trip.'

Harry laughed and Emma wanted to close her eyes and soak up the sound and save it for later. 'Don't worry, we're pretty good at what we do. All of us pilots have years of experience.'

'Where are you going tomorrow? Is there a proper landing strip?'

Harry nodded. Beside the door a large map had been

attached to the wall. The map was liberally studded with coloured pins. He pointed to a pin. 'To White Cliffs.'

'Would I be working?' She wasn't sure that she wanted to be thrown in at the deep end and it seemed like that would be the case if she took this job. She didn't know if she was ready for the challenge just yet. She'd come to Australia for a break, a chance to take stock of her life. Diving into this job might not be the best way of sorting herself out. She'd vowed to return to nursing but it didn't have to happen tomorrow.

'I'm sure you could help out if you wanted to. It's Kerri's last day before she starts maternity leave so I imagine you'd really just be a spare pair of hands.'

The distance on the map between Broken Hill and White Cliffs was only a few centimetres. It didn't look far and Emma wondered why they needed to fly. 'How far is it?'

'About three hundred kilometres. It takes a little over half an hour to fly but nearly three hours to drive.'

'It doesn't look that far.'

Harry ran his fingers around a black line that was drawn on the map. 'This is the area we cover—it's the size of France.'

'You're kidding.' Emma was amazed. She knew Australia was a vast continent but she really hadn't grasped the concept. 'All that way in those little planes?'

'Have you been in a small plane before?' Harry was looking at her carefully. 'And I mean really small.'

Emma nodded. 'I grew up around planes. My father was a doctor in the air force.'

Harry visibly relaxed. 'The planes might be a bit different from what you're used to but I'm sure they have one thing in common, which is state-of-the-art technology. Do you want to see inside one?'

'Sure.'

Harry punched some numbers into a numeric keypad and pushed open the door. Emma followed him through into the hangar. It was an impressive structure. Immaculately clean and organised and enormous, its size completely dwarfed the little plane that sat on the polished concrete floor. Emma followed Harry across the floor. The plane had looked small from the doorway but she had assumed it was just because the hangar was so large, but up close it was just as tiny.

Harry climbed in first. He was wearing dark blue overalls, a flightsuit similar to what RAF pilots wore, and as he ducked his head to get through the doorway the overalls tightened across his buttocks, treating her to a very pleasant picture. Harry turned just inside the door and stretched out his hand to help her up the steps. There was only one way to find out if the plane really was as small as it looked. Emma reached up and clasped his hand. It was warm and strong and huge and her hand disappeared inside his palm.

She let him help her into the plane and she almost ended up in his arms before he swivelled out of her way. There wasn't much room to manoeuvre and she was still close enough to notice his scent. He smelt of sunshine, of fresh air and the outdoors. He smelt the way clean clothes smelt when you brought the washing inside on a summer's day. He smelt perfect and Emma wished she could bottle his scent and save it to take back to England. It would be just the thing to bring a smile to her face on a cold, grey winter's afternoon.

While she was daydreaming about bottling sunshine Harry had let go of her hand and turned to sit on one of the seats. He swivelled it round so that it faced the back of the plane, and her. She was almost five feet ten inches tall and there wasn't enough head room inside the plane for her to stand upright, let alone Harry, so she sat down opposite him. Her knees brushed against his as she sat and even through the fabric she was aware of his body heat.

Something about him stirred her senses. She was acutely aware of him. Her hormones were definitely re-acting to his pheromones and she was aware of a spark of attraction—not that she would act on it, at least not here. She didn't think it was just her teenage dreams running away with her imagination but regardless she needed to focus. She gathered her thoughts and turned her attention to Harry's words and what he was telling her about the plane.

It was compact and very well organised. All the famil-iar medical equipment was there, carefully stowed or se-cured in place. Running along one side of the plane was a stretcher attached to a hydraulic arm and a row of single seats, positioned one behind the other, ran down the length of the plane on the opposite side of the extremely narrow aisle. There wasn't an inch of wasted space in this mini emergency room.

She closed her eyes as she tried to imagine what it would be like to work in this environment. It was dif-ficult to envisage but it was probably exactly what she needed to get her back into nursing. It was so far removed from anything she was familiar with that there would be no danger of triggering memories of working in London. It was perfect.

'Are you all right?' Harry's voice broke her concen-tration. 'You don't suffer from claustrophobia, do you?'

Emma opened her eyes and found herself looking di-rectly into Harry's blue gaze. He was leaning forward, mere inches from her, and he had a worried look on his face. 'God no.' She laughed. 'Can you imagine?'

She forced herself to look around the plane as if she was taking stock of the confined space but in reality she had to force herself to look away from Harry. It had been only yesterday that she'd told Sophie she was finished with dating but sitting this close to Harry, looking into his blue eyes, breathing in his scent, she knew her body had other ideas. She needed to get her raging hormones under control before they got her into trouble.

'So, what do you think?' he asked. 'Can you see yourself working in here?'

'Actually, I can,' she replied. It would be a challenging job, there was no doubt about that, but she had a feeling a challenge was just what she needed.

'Excellent. Irene'll be stoked.'

'Stoked?'

'Pleased,' he clarified.

And what about you? Emma wanted to know. *Will you be 'stoked' too?* But even if she'd been brave enough to ask, the moment was lost as an alarm sounded.

'What is that for?' she asked.

'It means we've been called out on a flight. I'll have to go,' he said as he stood up, well, not stood exactly, rather unfolded himself as much as possible, leaving Emma to wonder again how he managed to fit into the cockpit. There must be more space up the front than she pictured. He was leaning over her, no doubt waiting for her to move so he could get out. She hustled out of her seat and down the steps, where she was surprised to find Irene waiting for her.

'I'll take you back to the offices, Emma,' Irene said. 'You can't be out here unaccompanied.'

'You should come with us tomorrow,' Harry suggested. 'Get Irene to organise it and I'll see you in the morning.'

There was no time to argue, there was no time to do

anything except watch as Harry was collected by two other people who Emma assumed were the duty doctor and the flight nurse and raced out of the hangar.

Emma frowned and glanced at the plane that sat on the concrete beside her, the one she'd just climbed out of. 'Where are they going?' she asked Irene.

'This is the standby plane. There's a plane out on the apron, ready to go. It takes too long to get the plane out of the hangar, there's no time for that in an emergency. As soon as the plane has been unloaded and restocked it's put back on the apron ready for the next job.'

As Irene finished speaking Emma could hear a mechanical whine as the twin turbo propellers started up and then she saw the plane taxiing past the hangar doors.

'Why don't we go and finish this process? If you're keen to go out with the team tomorrow, I'll need to get some paperwork completed.'

A big part of Emma wanted to be on that plane right now. She loved the adrenalin buzz she got from working in an emergency department and she could just imagine how that was probably magnified a hundred times if the emergency was in an unfamiliar or foreign setting. Every job the flying doctor went to would be different. No two jobs the same. How incredible would that be?

She wanted to work here, she realised. The drama, challenges and variety appealed to her sense of adventure. She missed nursing and she had a feeling the flying doctor service might suit her very well.

She watched as the plane, piloted by Harry, soared off the runway and flew off into the clear blue sky. Tomorrow, she resolved, she'd be on that plane.

Harry almost had a visual on White Cliffs now. The flight had been uneventful, the weather perfect for flying, and

Emma had kept a running commentary going as she'd peered through the aircraft window at the ground below. She hadn't shown any sign of nerves as they'd prepared to take off that morning and judging from the excited tone in her voice she was feeling quite comfortable, despite the fact that the last time she'd been in a relatively small plane things hadn't gone so well. Harry hoped he could manage to execute a smoother landing for her today.

He could hear every word of her commentary over his headset and he didn't need to see her in the back of the plane to be able to picture her face. She was laughing at the sight of a flock of emus racing across the plains and in his mind's eye he could see her matching dimples flashing in her cheeks. Her long brown hair had been secured in a plait and it would be hanging down her back as she pressed her face to the glass.

'What about kangaroos, Harry? When will I see them?'

'Dawn and dusk is the time to spot 'roos,' he told her. 'They don't come out in the heat of the day, they'll be resting under the trees.'

'What are those white hills? Are they ants' nests? They're huge.'

Through the cockpit window Harry could see the hills Emma was referring to. They weren't ants' nests. 'They're the mullock heaps,' he explained. 'White Cliffs is a mining town and the piles of white are the soil that's been excavated and brought up from below by the miners. You should be able to see lots of holes in the ground now, which are the mine shafts.'

The red dirt was dotted with myriad white mounds of white shale, which always reminded Harry of mini-volcanoes. He could picture Emma's green eyes sparkling as she searched the ground for the landmarks he was telling her to watch out for.

'I can. They're perfect little circles, hundreds of them. It looks like we're flying over the moon.'

She was right, there was something rather alien and lunar about the landscape. 'They reckon there are over fifty thousand mine shafts around here, so watch where you walk.'

'Old mines aren't sealed off?' Emma asked.

'Not usually.'

'What do they mine here?'

'Opals,' Harry said as he guided the plane down to the airport runway in a near perfect landing.

'Opals! My birthstone is opal,' Emma said as Harry brought the plane to a stop.

'Really? Well we might have to see if we can show you some.'

'Today?'

'Maybe,' he replied as they began to load gear into the back of a four-wheel-drive vehicle that had come out to meet them. 'Shall I see if I can borrow a car at lunchtime so I can take you for a quick tour of the town? It's an interesting place.'

'I'd like that,' she said as she climbed into the back seat of the four-wheel drive with Grace, leaving the roomier front seat for Kerri and her swollen, pregnant stomach.

Harry waved them off and Emma waved back as Grace began to fill her in on the day's schedule.

'What happens now?' Emma asked.

'The clinic is held in the community health centre. There will be a flexible booking system. We tend to see the more urgent cases first—we need to get them seen to just in case we get called out on an emergency.'

'What happens to the people who don't get seen?'

'There are local nurses who take care of basic health care like ante- and postnatal care, immunisations, health screenings and the like so they can manage anything that's not too complicated. If necessary, people can access more comprehensive services in Wilcannia. We only visit White Cliffs three times a month but we're in Wilcannia four times a week and there are inpatient facilities there too. It's only about a hundred kilometres away.'

That was a long way in an emergency, Emma thought, but she didn't have time to dwell on it. She was well occupied once they got under way with everything from ultrasounds on expectant mothers to applying a cast to a teenager who'd broken his arm the week before. He'd had a backslab applied in Wilcannia but now that the swelling had subsided he needed something more restrictive.

Emma could scarcely believe she was actually working as a nurse again. She'd been in Broken Hill for less than thirty-six hours and complete strangers had convinced her to get back to work. A week ago she wouldn't have thought it was possible that not only would she return to nursing but that she would be enjoying it. She hadn't realised how much she'd missed it. And even though this wasn't quite the fast-paced emergency work she was used to, it felt like a step in the right direction.

She smiled to herself as she finished off the boy's cast and washed her hands. She'd thought she would have plenty of time to recover from the trials of the past twelve months while she was here, she'd thought time would go slowly in the back of beyond, but it seemed she'd been mistaken. But being busy might just be the best thing to happen to her. Being busy might be the answer to putting herself back together again and feeling like the person she used to be.

Next on her list was a fifty-year-old miner who presented with a deep gash on his left forearm. In Emma's opinion it should have been sutured two days earlier when the accident had happened but her patient hadn't seen the urgency. He'd simply bandaged it up himself and continued working.

'I only called in here because I had to come into town for supplies,' he told her as she cleaned and rebandaged the wound. Perhaps that's what happened when medical care wasn't easy to come by, she thought. People just got on with things. She taped the end of the bandage and was about to give him a precautionary anti-tetanus injection when she heard Harry's voice.

She didn't find it surprising that his deep drawl was recognisable to her after only a couple of days. Already she felt as though she'd been in the Outback much longer. While her surroundings were still unfamiliar, she didn't feel out of place. She was as comfortable here in the middle of nowhere as she'd ever been in England.

She could hear Harry's voice getting closer and as she pulled off her gloves and gave the miner his last-minute instructions Harry and Grace appeared by her side.

'It's a bit early for lunch, isn't it?' she asked.

'We have an emergency,' Grace said.

CHAPTER FOUR

'AN EMERGENCY?' Emma repeated.

Grace nodded. 'A farmer has come off his motorbike and it sounds like he has a compound femoral fracture. We're the closest available team. We need to get out to him.'

'Did you want me to continue on here while you head off?' Emma assumed that's what Grace would want but she was shaking her head.

'No. It's a bit more complicated than that. Can you come with us? We'll explain on the way.'

'Okay.' Emma quickly threw her gloves and the other rubbish into the bin and headed for the door. Harry fell into step beside her while Grace stopped to talk to Kerri.

'So what's the complication?' Emma asked Harry.

'The airstrip on the station is dirt and because of recent floods the strip is still too wet to land on.'

'So are we driving?'

'No. The station is only about a hundred kilometres east of here as the crow flies but it's a good two-hour drive. It doesn't sound as if the patient has got that amount of time. We have to fly.'

Emma wasn't following the conversation. 'But—'

'We've got a chopper coming in from another station to pick us up and fly us out there.'

Grace caught back up to them. 'Okay, let's get going.' She'd collected a couple of medical kits and Emma and Harry helped load these into the car. Emma expected them to wait for Kerri and she was surprised to find Harry driving away without the other nurse.

'What about Kerri?' she asked.

'Kerri won't have room to manoeuvre in the chopper. It's not designed for heavily pregnant women,' Harry said as he drove the car back to the airport.

'And we won't have any lifting equipment to load the patient into the chopper either, which would be a risk for Kerri,' Grace elaborated. 'She'll stay with the clinic until we know what the situation is. We'll either chopper the patient out to Wilcannia or if he needs to go to Adelaide we'll transfer him to the plane here. Either way, we'll come back for Kerri and depending what the time is we'll make a decision on the clinic then. That's why I want you to come. I need your help.'

There wasn't time to protest, and Emma had no intention of refusing to go anyway. She was about to experience authentic flying doctor work. She was starting to think she could get used to this job. For someone who tried to avoid making plans, unforeseen changes to her schedule weren't a problem and she thought the variety would suit her very well.

When they reached the airport Emma saw a chopper sitting on the dirt beside the flying doctor plane, its blades spinning slowly.

'Grace, if you and Emma can grab what we need I'll work out the flight plan with Neil. Give me a yell if you need a hand.'

'Harry's not flying the chopper, is he?' Emma asked Grace.

'No, he's coming as the navigator.'

Everything was happening very quickly and Emma had no option but to follow Grace's lead and help out where she could. Grace quickly selected supplies and then Emma helped her to load the stretcher into the helicopter. It was a tight squeeze once the stretcher was laid across the floor and Emma had to sit with her legs crossed and her feet on the seat. Grace was straight onto the radio to communicate with the injured farmer's wife so by the time they landed at the station they would have an idea of what they would be dealing with.

Chris had been out checking his sheep but because of the recent rains and floods east of Broken Hill and White Cliffs, the grass was high and his vision had been obscured. He'd collided with a sheep and been thrown over the handlebars of his motorbike. He'd apparently tried to stand up, only to see bone sticking through the fabric of his trousers. He had been out of radio contact as the radio had been taken into Broken Hill for repairs yet somehow he'd managed to get back on his quad bike and travel, very slowly, the seven kilometres back to the house, where he was now in the care of his wife, Ros.

'Is he bleeding a lot?' Grace asked.

'No. I've put a tourniquet around his thigh but he's in a lot of pain.'

Emma didn't doubt that and she noticed Grace gave a wry smile in response to Ros's comment.

Grace kept chatting to Ros and Chris as the chopper made its way east. There was nothing for Emma to do except listen and look at the view, through the windows. It changed as they travelled away from White Cliffs. They crossed a river, swollen after recent rains, and the surrounding land was marked by secondary flood channels and interspersed with green grass. The country was beautiful and not at all what she'd imagined the Australian Outback to look like. In contrast to the greyish-green colour of the flora around Broken Hill, the land out here looked lush and most definitely green. But as unexpected as it was, it couldn't keep her attention.

She could see Harry in profile, where he sat beside the chopper pilot, and her focus kept drifting away from the windows and to Harry. She could see where his hair curled slightly above his ears. He had very nice earlobes, but it was his jaw that caught her attention. Strong, square and masculine, it suited him.

'We're almost with you.' Grace's comment through the headset brought Emma's attention back to the matter at hand. She needed to focus, needed to put Harry to the back of her mind.

Within minutes they were on the ground. Emma and Grace grabbed an emergency pack each and ducked low to avoid the chopper's blades as they ran to the house.

The house was elevated on short stilts that lifted it a few feet above the ground. Chris was lying in the mud at the foot of the stairs, his quad bike inches away, his wife kneeling beside him, clutching his hand. It was clear Chris hadn't been able to make it any further. He must have collapsed when he reached the house and fallen off his bike and that's where he'd stayed.

Emma had been worried about working away from a hospital environment but when she saw Chris lying in the dirt, injured and in pain, she realised the location didn't matter. It was secondary to the drama. All that mattered was attending to Chris and getting him stable enough to move. All that mattered was saving a life.

He was pale and sweaty, his eyes were glazed. His shirt was streaked with vomit and his trousers were torn and bloodstained. His right leg lay at an unnatural angle with his femur fractured in two. He wasn't in good shape.

They might not be in an emergency department or a sterile operating suite but Emma knew what she had to do. Her job.

'I'll do his obs,' she said as she unzipped an emergency pack and pulled out a sphygmomanometer and the oximeter, leaving Grace to start her assessment.

'Pain out of ten?' Grace asked.

'Ten,' Chris answered. His voice was barely audible over the noise of the helicopter, and the effort it took him to get that one word out was obvious.

'BP eighty on fifty. Pulse one-forty. Oxygen ninety-eight per cent.' Emma relayed her readings as she reached for a bag of saline and began to prepare a drip.

Harry appeared beside her and reached for the saline bag. 'Let me hold that for you,' he said.

'Are you sure?'

'I won't faint at the sight of a bit of blood, if that's what you're worried about,' he replied with a smile. 'We're bred tougher than that out here. Think of me as an extra pair of hands. You'll find I can be pretty useful.'

Emma finished inserting the canula and got the drip flowing then passed the bag to Harry. He held it above Chris, and Emma could tell he'd done the same thing many times before.

'Can you draw up twenty milligrams of morphine too? I think it's best if we sedate him before we try to move,' Grace said, when she saw what Emma was doing. 'Then we'll splint his leg and get him in the chopper. He needs to go to Adelaide.'

Emma drew up the morphine and, out of habit, held it out for Grace to check before she administered it through the drip. She was aware of Harry standing behind her, waiting patiently for them to finish attending to Chris. She could feel the air around them crackling with electricity and her skin was tingling. But she still had work to do. She had to block Harry from her mind; she had to ignore her crazy reaction to his presence.

Grace had cut through the leg of Chris's trousers and the extent of the damage he'd done was plain for everyone to see. Emma couldn't resist glancing at Harry, seeking his reaction. She was surprised to find him smiling at her.

'I told you there's no need to worry about me. I've broken my fair share of bones and had more stitches than I care to remember.'

He certainly looked fine. More than fine, she thought as she turned back to help Grace. She poured an antiseptic wash over the wound before padding the fracture site and fixing an inflatable splint around Chris's leg. Harry had brought the stretcher across earlier and had left it on a tarpaulin that he'd spread over the muddy ground. As she and Grace prepared to roll Chris onto the stretcher, Harry handed the drip to Chris's wife and squatted down beside Emma. His forearm brushed against hers as he knelt in the mud and Emma's pulse beat a little faster.

'What are you doing?' she asked.

'I'll help you roll him. Grace can slide the stretcher under and then we're good to go.'

Harry was calm and matter-of-fact and his relaxed demeanour was reassuring. On the count of three they rolled Chris towards them on his left side as Grace positioned the stretcher before they rolled him smoothly back.

She and Harry lifted Chris and loaded him into the chopper while Grace carried the drip. Harry was right. Having an extra pair of hands made all the difference out in the middle of nowhere. He was able to lift, carry or hold whatever they needed and his size and strength made everything look easy. As Emma and Grace settled Chris into the chopper ready for the flight Harry packed up the medical kits and stowed them on board.

Emma was impressed at how well co-ordinated the team was. She even felt like she'd contributed to a successful retrieval. She didn't feel like the new kid on the block. She felt good. Getting back into nursing felt like the right thing to be doing.

Every minute on the short flight was spent trying to keep Chris alive. Emma was aware of Harry in her peripheral vision but she had no time on the return journey to watch him.

Kerri was waiting for them at the little airport in White Cliffs and as quickly and smoothly as possible the team transferred Chris to the plane for the flight to Adelaide.

'That was a baptism by fire,' Harry said to her as she buckled herself into the co-pilot's seat. Grace and Kerri would monitor Chris on this flight and Emma was relieved to hand over her responsibilities. Not because she liked the alternative option, which was sitting up the front with Harry, well, not only because of that, but because she was exhausted.

The cockpit was as small as she'd imagined. Harry kept reaching in front of her as he fiddled with controls and prepared for take-off, and each time he leaned across her she breathed in deeply, inhaling his scent. He smelt wonderful. Emma suspected she did not. The uniform she was wearing was filthy, covered in blood and splattered with mud while, once again, Harry was pristine and immaculate. How was it that she was the one who always ended up looking a mess?

'How are you feeling?' he asked.

'Worn out,' she replied. 'But happy. It was a good outcome.' She yawned and stretched, encouraging air into her lungs and blood to her brain in an effort to keep herself awake. 'How does everyone manage to keep up the pace?' she asked as Harry pulled back on the controls and the plane left the runway.

'I think the adrenalin keeps everyone going. There's no time to think about how tired you are until after the patient has been taken care of and in this case it'll be hours before we get down to Adelaide and back again.'

'We'll be back today?'

'Yep.'

'That's a long day for you, having to fly us back again.'

'I'm used to it.'

'Do you love it?'

'What?'

'Your job.'

'I love flying,' he replied honestly. He did love flying but if he was going to be honest he'd admit that he found the clinic runs monotonous. There was too much time spent sitting around in his opinion and not enough time flying. He preferred the excitement and variety required when he had to fly the team to emergencies.

His ideal job would be running Connor's Corner, the family cattle station, but that was his brother's domain and Emma didn't need to hear his feelings on that topic. He didn't want to talk about his life.

'You did a terrific job with Chris,' he told her. 'You and Grace worked well together.'

Emma turned towards him and smiled broadly. Her green eyes were shining and her dimples flashed in her cheeks, and Harry made a mental note to compliment her more often.

'I'm sorry you didn't get to see anything of the town, though,' he added.

She shrugged. 'No matter. I'm glad I got to go out for the emergency. It gave me a taste of real flying doctor medicine and I preferred it to the clinic session, it's actually more similar to the work I'm used to. I think I prefer the challenge of an emergency.'

Harry knew the feeling. Emma's sentiments echoed his. There was nothing quite like challenging yourself, pushing your own boundaries and seeing how good you could be.

'Perhaps I can bring you back to White Cliffs on the weekend. What do you think? Do you have plans?'

'No, I don't, I'm not big on plans. But I'm not sure if Sophie's made any arrangements. Can we wait and see?'

'Of course.' He was disappointed that she hadn't leapt at his invitation but what should he expect? He needed to remember that she had an aversion to making plans. At least he hoped that was her reason. He'd rethink his approach and try again. 'It's no problem.'

Harry had refuelled and prepared the plane for the return trip from Adelaide to Broken Hill and was waiting for the team to finish their patient handover when he saw Grace striding towards him.

She stopped one pace from him. 'You're not wasting any time.'

'What are you talking about?'

'Inviting Emma out to White Cliffs.'

Harry didn't need to ask how she knew. His conversation with Emma had been conducted through the headsets of the plane so Grace would have heard every word.

'Do you think it's wise?' she asked.

'What?'

'I know she's just your type but she's Sophie's cousin.'

'My type?' Harry was intrigued. He didn't realise he had a 'type'. 'What exactly is my type?'

'Attractive brunettes with long legs. But, most importantly, they're always transient.'

'What do you mean by that?'

'I've known you, what? Three years? And you've only ever dated girls who are here for a specific, and by that I mean short, stay. No one local. No one who might like to stick around and make your life difficult.'

'Is that what you think?'

'Yes. You're not going to tell me I'm wrong, are you?' Grace asked. 'But just be careful. After Emma's performance today I'm hoping we can persuade her to consider volunteering to cover for Kerri until Lisa is back in action. I don't want you jeopardising that. It can be dangerous playing so close to home.'

Harry had to admit Grace had a point but he was willing to risk her wrath, just this once. In his opinion it was always a good day when an attractive woman arrived in town and he wasn't going to pass up the chance to spend time with Emma if she was willing.

Her long legs, sparkling green eyes and flashing dimples were a combination he found hard to resist and if she had no objections to accompanying him back to White Cliffs he wasn't about to let Grace talk him out of it. 'I'm just offering to show her the sights. It's all perfectly innocent.'

Grace laughed. 'I've seen you in action, Harry Connor, and innocent does not describe you. You have a way of getting what you want and making the women think it was all their idea.'

Harry grinned. 'If they come willingly, I'm not about to argue. Emma might like a bit of old-fashioned country hospitality.'

Grace laughed. 'Is that what you're calling it these days?'

'Yes, as a matter of fact.'

Grace was shaking her head at him but he could see

more laughter bubbling up behind her dark eyes. 'When are you going to settle down, Harry? You can't play around for ever.'

'Don't try and ruin my fun. There's no point even thinking about settling down until I find somewhere to settle,' he told her.

He had to pretend all he wanted was to have fun. If Grace or anyone knew how much he longed to settle down he'd never hear the end of it, but he'd meant what he'd told Grace. First he needed somewhere to settle, then he'd worry about finding someone to settle with. He had a picture of his ideal partner in his mind but until he had something to offer he was in no hurry to go and find her. Until he had something to offer he intended to have as much fun as possible. And if Emma was up for it, he was happy to include her in his merriment.

Harry was at Emma's door early on Saturday morning. Not early enough to be considered rude but early enough to make sure she wouldn't have gone elsewhere. He waited for what seemed like ages for the door to be answered. Just as he was starting to wonder if he was too late, Emma greeted him with her megawatt smile and flashing dimples. A feeling of delightful anticipation swept over him.

'Harry! What are you doing here?'

She looked fresh and lovely and had obviously just climbed out of bed. She was wearing pyjamas and her eyes were luminous and green. Harry imagined that was exactly how she'd look after she'd just been thoroughly satisfied and it was all he could do to stop himself from taking her in his arms right then and there and kissing her soundly. In just a few days she'd captured his attention completely.

'Have you ever slept underground?' he asked her.

'Have I what?'

'Ever slept underground? It's an amazing experience, so quiet and peaceful, almost as good as sleeping miles from anywhere under the stars. I'm here to see if you'd like to come back to White Cliffs with me for the weekend. There's an underground motel there, I've reserved two rooms—you said you don't like making plans, so I was hoping this invitation might be spontaneous enough for you.'

'It's not about being spontaneous. It's just that whenever I make plans something seems to go wrong,' she replied. She looked over his shoulder at the people walking in the street. She stepped back, out of the doorway. 'You'd better come in.'

He followed her down the passage into the open-plan kitchen at the rear of the house.

'How do you know I don't have other plans?' she asked.

Harry laughed. 'There aren't too many secrets in this town.'

'Oh, I'd been hoping for anonymity.'

'That will only be a temporary status,' he told her. He smiled and admitted a little guiltily, 'To be honest, Sophie told me she's rostered on at the hospital this weekend and she asked me to keep you company, and I figured, seeing as you don't like to make plans, that I'd take a chance and be spontaneous. So what do you think? Would you like to come with me?'

She stood still, silent, considering. He couldn't believe how nervous he was. How badly he was hoping to hear her say yes.

'What are we going to do there?'

Was that a 'yes'?

'A friend of mine is just about to open a tourist mine. I thought we could go fossicking to see if we can find your birthstone.'

She smiled at him again and his heart pounded in his chest. 'What do I need to pack?'

A definite 'yes'! 'Nothing fancy but you'll need something warm for the evening.'

'Okay, give me five minutes.'

When she returned she'd changed out of her pyjamas and into very short shorts and a sleeveless top. Just as he'd suspected, she had magnificent legs, long and toned and tanned. She was wearing canvas sneakers and in one hand she held a broad-brimmed sunhat and in the other she carried a small bag. It was a tenth of the size of the duffel bag he'd carried for her on the day they'd met.

'Is that all?' he teased.

He was rewarded with another smile and he decided her could get used to seeing her dimples.

'I didn't think I'd need four pairs of shoes for one night away,' she told him.

He took her bag from her and loaded it into the boot of his four-wheel drive while Emma left a note for Sophie. She knew Soph wouldn't mind—in fact, she was pretty sure Soph would have insisted she accept Harry's invitation.

But Sophie wasn't there and Emma told herself that was why she was going to White Cliffs because it was preferable to spending the weekend alone while Sophie worked. She wanted to see as much of the country as possible and the fact that Harry was offering to be her tour guide was a bonus.

She couldn't deny she was attracted to him but she was certain she could keep her hormones under control for two days. Besides, he'd given no indication that the invitation was anything but friendly. She could do friendly.

'Who is this mate of yours with the opal mine?' Emma asked once they were on the road, heading out of town.

She was intrigued with the idea of meeting someone who mined opals but more intrigued with the prospect of meeting one of Harry's friends.

'Tony and I were at boarding school together. He was always coming up with ways to make money—it started with him selling our boarding-house lunches to the day students and at the moment it's him excavating an opal mine for tourists. He's originally from rural South Australia but he caught the opal-mining bug one holiday when he came to stay with my family.'

'Your family is from White Cliffs?'

'Apart from the Aborigines no one in Australia is really from anywhere local, particularly in the case of mining towns. Every family still talks about where they came from originally. In my case it was Ireland. My great-grandfather ended up in White Cliffs and made his fortune with opals. He then bought land north of here and started a cattle station. That's where I grew up but we spent some time here as kids just fossicking.'

'Who's on the station now?'

'My parents still live there but my brother runs it.'

'Is it far from here?'

'Not really, about seven hundred kilometres or nine hours on dirt roads, as long as there's no flooding.'

Emma laughed. 'That's not far?'

'Not out here it's not.'

Harry was pleased she'd agreed to spend the weekend with him. He was keen for her to see something of his place for he was part of this country just as it was part of him. He knew he wanted everyone to feel empathy and awe and wonder for what he believed was the most amazing place on earth and he loved getting the chance to show people the beauty of this sometimes harsh and unforgiving land. Emma, he suspected, would appreciate the majesty of the Outback.

It was still very much a wild frontier and it suited people like Emma, people who didn't like to make plans, people who Harry thought would benefit from being away from regimented city life. He also had a feeling she was searching for answers and there was every chance she'd find them here.

The scenery was unchanging for mile after mile and Emma was beginning to lose track of how long they'd been travelling when she finally saw the road signs welcoming them to White Cliffs. But Harry ignored the signs pointing to the town centre and instead turned off onto a side road marked 'Tourist Trail'.

'Tony's expecting us about now so we'll call at his place first and then go on to the motel,' he told her as he negotiated the dirt road.

Emma assumed he was following the green tourist trail signs, although it was quite possible that he knew where he was going, but how anyone could tell one turn from another out here was anyone's guess.

The road wound around several mullock heaps and Emma held her breath, hoping there wasn't an unmarked mine shaft in their path that was large enough to cause a problem. From the air it had been easy to spot the myriad mine shafts but from this perspective it was much harder and quite disconcerting. But Harry's posture was relaxed. He seemed to know what he was doing and Emma trusted him.

Eventually Harry slowed and pulled to a stop beside an old winch. The buckets hanging from the chain had long since rusted but a new sign had been fixed to the metal frame: 'White Cliffs Tourist Mine—experience the underground life of an opal miner.'

'This is it,' Harry said as he climbed out of the four-wheel drive.

Emma stepped out of the car and looked around. There was nothing that distinguished this spot from a dozen others around them, save for the sign.

'Where do we go?' she asked.

'Down there,' Harry said, as he pointed behind the sign to a long slope that disappeared around a corner. The slope was wide enough to take a vehicle and down one side of it a flight of wide steps had been cut into the red dirt.

Emma followed Harry to the steps but she mistimed the first step and slipped off the edge of it onto the second step. She caught her breath in surprise.

'Are you all right? Harry asked, as he reached for her hand, steadying her. 'We probably should have got you some sturdier shoes.'

'I'm fine,' she replied, but Harry slowed his pace and held onto her hand anyway as they descended into the cutting. Emma didn't protest. Harry's touch sent little flutters of excitement racing through her and she didn't want it to stop.

As they rounded a corner at the bottom of the cutting, the steps ended at a flattened area about twice the size of a double garage. The walls of red dirt towered above them and Emma figured they were about fifteen metres below surface level in what looked like a small quarry. She could see a doorway cut into the side of the quarry, which had been reinforced with thick wooden beams, and the door itself was ajar. A sign above the door repeated the information she'd read on the sign by the car.

'This all looks very civilised,' she said to Harry. The

steps and doorway were not what she'd expected. 'I had visions of having to climb down one of those skinny shafts.'

Harry laughed and Emma wanted to close her eyes and let the sound wash over her.

'Tony didn't want to make it too difficult for people to get to him so access has been simplified. He dug out this area so that small tour buses can drive right to the door and he's going to make a car park at the top that will be able to take the caravans and camper trailers favoured by the grey nomads.'

'Who are grey nomads?'

'That's the nickname for the people who spend their retirement driving around the country, seeing Australia. Once you're inside the mine the experience becomes a bit more authentic, you'll see.'

'Harry, good to see you, mate.' A solidly built man, who was slightly taller than her, came out of the mine to greet them. His salt-and-pepper hair was cut short and his jaw was covered with grey stubble. He was dressed in light brown cotton drill pants and matching shirt and on his feet were thick-soled workboots, probably just the type of thing she should be wearing, Emma thought.

'Tony!' Harry greeted his friend with a hug.

Finding out that Harry was a hugging type pleased Emma but it didn't surprise her. He seemed to be a warm, happy, genuine man, just the type who would hug his mates, but again very different from most of the men Emma knew and totally different from her ex. It made her feel good to spend time with someone like Harry.

Sophie was right. It was hard to be miserable out here but it wasn't because of the weather. It was because of Harry.

'Emma, this is Tony. Tony, Emma.' Harry interrupted her rambling thoughts.

'Welcome, welcome,' Tony said, and kissed her on both cheeks, European style, catching her slightly off guard.

'Hello, Tony, very nice to meet you,' she said, thinking that Tony's kisses didn't send a tingle through her like the touch of Harry's hand did.

'Emma, Emma, you're just what I need, a real tourist.'

Emma wondered why everyone seemed so surprised to hear her English accent. Harry had just finished telling her how everyone here had come from somewhere else and Tony himself looked as though he had European heritage, Italian or possibly Greek. Surely they were used to visitors, wasn't that why Tony was working on this project?

'Come in,' he said. 'You're perfect for my market research. I'm almost ready to open to the public so I want your honest opinion on everything you see today.'

Tony led them through the doorway and the red cliff face opened into a large room that he had styled as a visitors' centre. Newspaper articles and pictures depicting the history of White Cliffs were displayed on the walls, along with aerial photographs and maps plus descriptions of the different types of opal found throughout Australia and what was found in the White Cliffs area. Despite being underground, the room was well lit and a flat-screen television was mounted on one wall. Emma could hear the distant hum of a generator in the background.

'This looks fantastic, Tony.'

He was bouncing around like an excited schoolboy. 'My friends who run the cafés and art galleries and souvenir shops have been saying for years that all the tourists ask if there's a mine they can visit. There's been nothing so I decided to build one. I'm going to show a video of how opal is mined today and then through this archway people can travel back in time to see what the working conditions were like fifty years ago.'

'Can we see it? Is it ready?'

'It's almost ready. If you'd like to see it, I can show you.'

He picked up two bright yellow hard hats from a shelving unit behind a counter and passed them to Emma and Harry. 'You'll need to wear these,' he said as he put his own on his head. 'Occupational health and safety requirements.'

Through the archway was a passage, high enough for even Harry to stand upright in. Lights were strung along one wall and behind panes of Perspex set into the wall Emma could see seams of opal.

'This spot isn't rich in deposits,' Tony said, 'but I've displayed some of what I've found so people can see what it looks like in the rock. A bit further along there's an area where people can have a go at digging for opal.'

'And what if they get lucky?' Emma asked.

'It'd be unlikely.' Tony grinned. 'The geologists reckon this area is pretty well mined and I think most tourists wouldn't recognise unpolished opal if it fell into their laps.'

Emma put her hands on her hips in mock indignation and turned to Harry. 'Harry Connor, you got me here under false pretences! You said we'd be fossicking for my birthstone.'

'In that case, anything the two of you can dig up is yours, Emma. It wouldn't do for Harry to look bad,' Tony told her as they continued walking.

Emma could see why Harry and Tony had remained such firm friends, they both had the same smooth, swift charm about them. Above their heads a mine shaft stretched to the surface, the blue sky just visible at the top. A ladder ran the height of the shaft, reaching for the sky, and past the mine shaft the passage widened again into a large circular cavern. Replica lanterns hung from the walls and their light flickered convincingly. Small picks hung on chains from the walls. 'This marks the point where we go backwards in time,' Tony said.

Past the cavern the passage continued but it was half the height of before.

'What's down there?' Emma pointed towards the low-ceilinged tunnel.

'That's going to be a display tunnel showing working conditions of the early opal miners. Because everything they dug was by hand, they only dug large spaces if they were chasing an opal seam, otherwise it was a waste of energy. Most likely they would have been working on their knees.'

The lights flickered again and briefly went out, plunging them into darkness. Emma instinctively pressed closer to Harry, taking comfort in his warmth and size. She felt him move his arm and she was certain he was about to wrap it around her but then the lights shone again and his arm stayed by his side.

'I'd better go and check the generator,' Tony said. 'You're welcome to stay here and have a go with the picks. Harry will show you what to do.'

Emma looked at Harry. Who wouldn't want to hide away in a dimly lit room with him?

Harry ran his hand lightly over the surface of the wall. His fingers were long and slender and appeared to caress the rock. He traced his fingers over a line that ran across the wall a few feet from the floor.

'You need to look for lines in the rock. Opal tends to form on a fault line. You can quite easily chip away at the soft sandstone and you'll hear if you hit anything harder. Try here.'

Harry passed her a pick that was attached to the wall on a long chain. Emma chipped at the sandstone and the pick left gouge marks in the stone as though she'd run across it with a fork. The air underground was cool after the warmth of the sun at the surface and she shivered as her body temperature dropped.

'Are you cold?'

'A little.'

Harry rubbed her bare arms. The friction from his hands warmed her skin and heat flooded through her body. She felt it flow through her like a living thing, running through her belly and groin.

'Shall I go and fetch you another top from the car?' Harry asked.

Emma would have preferred him to stay and warm her with his hands but she didn't say that. How could she? *Friends. They were going to be friends*, she reminded herself. 'I'll be okay,' she said.

'It's no trouble. Will you be all right on your own for a few minutes? I'll be quick.'

She nodded. 'As long as the lights don't go out,' she said, and she smiled.

'I'll be right back.'

Harry was watching her closely and for a moment Emma thought he was going to lean in towards her. Was he going to kiss her? No, he just gave her arms another quick rub and disappeared along the passage, leaving her trying to prolong the sensation of the touch of his hands and wondering what she would have done if he had kissed her. She didn't think she would have resisted too vehemently. Actually, she doubted she would have resisted at all.

She moved further into the cavern, following the fault line that Harry had pointed out to her, and in the distance she heard a rumble that sounded like thunder. She was touching the wall and felt it vibrate under her hand in time with the noise. Dirt fell from the ceiling and little stones landed on her helmet, knocking it askew and making her jump.

As she reached up to adjust her hard hat she heard another rumble and this time she felt it through the floor of the cavern. The lights flickered again but although they stayed on, Emma felt nervous. She should have gone with Harry. She didn't like being alone at the best of times and she realised she liked it even less when she was underground. Surrounded by flickering lights and in complete silence, she felt very alone.

More debris fell from the roof and landed on the floor in front of her. She backed away, not wanting the dirt to fall on her safety helmet. She made a decision. She'd head out and meet Harry back at the entrance.

She was just about to make her way across the cavern when another rumble shook the mine and she watched in horror as one wall collapsed, trapping her on the wrong side of the mine exit. The exit was in front of her, on the other side of a pile of dirt.

Harry was on the other side of the pile of dirt.

She was totally alone.

The lights flickered again. Trapped underground.

By now she'd figured that there was blasting occurring somewhere on the opal fields and that was causing the damage, but what would happen if there was a fourth blast? What would happen if the ceiling came down on top of her?

She couldn't go forwards but behind her there was only the low-ceilinged tunnel and she had no idea if she'd be any safer in there. It would only take a small amount of falling debris to fill that tunnel.

She stood frozen to the spot. She couldn't go forwards and she didn't want to go backwards. Backwards would take her further into the mine and further away from Harry. He would come for her, wouldn't he?

But what if they were trapped too? She had no way of knowing where they were or if they were okay.

'Harry?' she tried calling, but her voice sounded muffled and pathetic as it was absorbed into the pile of dirt. She doubted it could be heard on the other side.

As she tried to fight back the first wave of panic, the lights flickered again.

Her heart was racing. She concentrated on breathing, counting her breaths, in, one, two, three, and out, one, two, three, while she thought about her options.

The lights flickered once more, plunging her into darkness. She waited—breathed in, breathed out—but the lights didn't come back on. It was pitch black, deadly silent and she was alone.

'Harry!'

She called out again, not expecting an answer, but any noise was preferable to the deafening silence that surrounded her in what felt like her solitary tomb.

CHAPTER FIVE

'EMMA?' Harry yelled. 'Emma, can you hear me?'

He had his hands on the pile of dirt that blocked their path as he waited for a reply. He was holding his breath, not daring to breathe in case the noise of his breathing prevented him from hearing Emma's voice. But there was nothing. Nothing but silence.

'She's on the other side of this?' Tony asked.

'She has to be,' he told Tony. She wasn't on their side and the alternative was that she was under the dirt and Harry wasn't prepared to contemplate that. He should never have left her alone.

He and Tony were standing under the old mine shaft with the cavern, or what remained of it, in front of them and a tiny portion of cloudless blue sky above. If only the collapse had occurred on this side of the shaft, Harry thought, Emma would have been able to climb out.

'There's another shaft,' Tony said. 'It's covered over but it leads down into the low tunnel on the far side of the cavern. We may be able to get to her that way.'

'Let's go.' Harry didn't hesitate and he refused to think Emma wouldn't be getting out.

Tony put his hand on Harry's forearm, holding him back. 'I think we should call the SAR team. They'll have the right equipment.'

'You can call them but I want you to show me where the mine shaft is. We can get it opened while we wait for the SAR team.' Harry knew that protocol probably meant that the White Cliffs Search and Rescue team should be involved, but if there was a way of getting down to Emma he had no intention of waiting, although he was prepared to go through the motions. He almost dragged Tony back to the entrance, demanding that he take him to the old shaft.

It was pitch black. And silent. There was not a sound. And it was as still as it was silent. There was no breeze.

Why would there be a breeze fifteen metres under the ground? she asked herself.

How long would the air last?

Hopefully as long as it took for someone to come for her, she thought. She refused to think that Harry wouldn't come.

She reached out one hand, wanting to feel the solid wall of the tunnel. She'd told Harry she didn't suffer from claustrophobia but that had been before she'd been buried alive. Feeling the wall gave her some comfort, some perspective, and grounded her. Perhaps she wasn't suffering from claustrophobia. If it was claustrophobia then surely feeling the wall behind her would reinforce the idea that she was trapped, but she found the solid wall comforting. Perhaps it was simply disorientation.

She laughed and the noise sounded harsh in the silence. There was nothing simple about this situation.

Maybe she was afraid of the dark or of being buried alive? Who wouldn't be afraid of being buried alive? Surely that was quite a rational, sane fear? She wondered what those phobias were called but she forced herself not to go down that path. She needed to be thinking positive thoughts, not naming fears.

There was no sound and no movement but at least that meant the blasting had stopped. That was a positive thing.

Gradually her eyes adjusted to the darkness and her gaze was drawn to her left, down the low-ceilinged tunnel. She could see tiny slivers of light in the distance.

She was drawn to the light like a moth to a flame. She needed that light.

She felt her way along the wall of the mine, reluctant to step away into the darkness, and followed the wall around until she reached the tunnel opening. It wasn't high enough to stand up in and she had to get on her hands and knees and crawl along. The dirt floor was rough against her skin and she could feel the little stones pressing into the soft skin of her palms and knees, but the light kept drawing her forwards.

For a long time the light didn't seem to get any closer and she wondered whether her eyes were playing tricks on her. But she pushed on. There was nothing else to do.

By the time she reached the light her knees were grazed and she was certain her palms were bleeding, but she'd made it. She found she was under another old shaft but when she looked up the opening was covered. There was no patch of blue sky at the top of this shaft, just tiny holes in a covering, emitting pinpricks of light. She stood up and searched the walls of the shaft for a ladder but could see nothing. She stood in the middle of the shaft and ran her hands around the wall just in case, but there was nothing but dirt. Light was coming in but there was still no way out. It wasn't an escape.

She was about to retrace her steps but when she looked at the darkness behind her she decided that the meagre bit of light coming down this boarded-up shaft was preferable to the pitch blackness that waited for her at the other end of the tunnel. It wasn't an escape route but at least there was air and some light. She sat cross-legged on the floor, her back to the wall, and waited for Harry.

Harry burst from the mine, still half dragging Tony with him, only letting him go once they were out in the fresh air. Tony pulled his mobile phone from his pocket and called the SAR team as they hurried up the steps to climb out of the cutting and emerge at ground level. Tony finished the call and stopped beside his utility vehicle.

He took a crowbar, an axe and two pairs of leather gloves from the tray of the ute and passed the crowbar and one pair of gloves to Harry. He paused for a moment as if to get his bearings.

'It's this way,' he said, before he headed north-east across the dirt road.

It was late afternoon and the sun was well on its way to the horizon but the heat of the day was still strong enough to be uncomfortable. They skirted mullock heaps and scrubby vegetation, keeping a vigilant eye out for any unmarked abandoned shafts. As the sunlight bounced off the hot, dry earth and the air shimmered around them Harry could taste the dust in the air. Their footsteps startled a flock of grey and yellow cockatiels that were feeding on the ground and they took to the skies in a flap of wings, screeching noisily.

Tony stopped beside a huge tyre that must have come from an excavator or bulldozer. Fixed across the tyre was an old wooden pallet topped with sheets of corrugated iron. The iron had rusted through in places, leaving dozens of small holes in the sheets.

Something passed across the top of the shaft, creating a shadow. Emma was vaguely aware of something blocking the light but before she could look up it had passed. Had she imagined it?

But there it was again and this time it was accompanied by a loud noise. Emma feared it was another blast and her initial reaction was to look for cover. But there was nowhere to hide. Then she realised the noise wasn't vibrating through the earth but instead it was echoing down the shaft. The noise was coming from above her.

'Hello, is someone up there? Can you hear me?'

'Emma?'

His voice was distorted as it bounced off the walls of the shaft but she knew it was Harry. No one else would know her name but it wasn't that, it was the fact that hearing her name on his lips made her heart somersault in her chest.

'Harry!'

He was coming for her.

'Are you hurt?'

'No. I'm fine. I'm just stuck. I can't get out.'

He was here. She hadn't doubted he would come for her.

'We'll have you out in a minute. We just need to get this cover off.'

Harry's words were drowned out by another bout of banging before the cover was levered off, the shaft was flooded with light and his head appeared above her. Even though she couldn't make out his features, just knowing he was there was all she needed.

'You're really okay?' he asked.

'Yes.' The word came out as a half laugh, half sob but it was pure relief that she felt.

'Okay, give me a second to work this out,' he said, and his head disappeared from the opening. She could hear him talking to Tony. 'There's a ladder running down the wall,' he said, and she knew he would choose to climb down to her.

Now that there was more light, she could see a rusty ladder but it stopped halfway down the shaft. A good six metres from the floor. He might be able to drop down to her but then they'd both be stuck. It wasn't going to help her. Or Harry.

'Harry, wait! The ladder doesn't reach the bottom,' she called.

'Don't worry, Em, we'll work something out,' Harry called down to her, even as Tony was arguing the point. Their voices drifted down the mine shaft.

'We should wait for Search and Rescue.'

'Why? You heard her, she's not injured, it's just a simple evacuation. We just need a way of getting down there. We can have her out before SAR even get here. What else have you got in your ute? Rope? Anything I can use as a harness?'

'There's rope and a winch on the front.'

'Can you bring it over?' Harry asked. 'I'll wait here, I'm not leaving Emma again.'

Despite her predicament Harry's words sent a warm glow through her. Harry was waiting. He wasn't going to leave her.

Emma heard the sound of the engine as Tony brought the ute closer. She could hear them working out how to fashion a rope harness for Harry and she could hear Tony trying once more to convince Harry to wait for the search and rescue team and then Harry insisting again that he could do this. Harry won the argument and Tony agreed to winch him down to her.

His face appeared at the top of the shaft again.

'Okay, Em, we're good to go. Can you slide out of the way into the tunnel a bit? I'm going to come down feet first so I won't have a good line of sight and I don't want to land on you.'

She scooted backwards into the tunnel and craned her neck so she could see what was going on. Her heart was in her throat as she watched him enter the shaft feet first. What if something happened to him?

Somehow, despite the makeshift harness, Tony managed to lower him steadily and smoothly. The moment his feet touched the bottom she leapt into his arms. The knotted harness rope and the winch cable dug into her stomach but she didn't care. Never in her life had she been so pleased to see someone.

Her knees were shaky and she clung to him, letting him support her. She'd managed to get off the ground and into his arms but she knew that she was now incapable of holding herself up. Adrenalin coursed through her system. She looked up into his bright blue eyes and her heart skipped a beat.

She saw his blue eyes darken before he tipped her hard hat back and claimed her lips with his mouth, kissing her swiftly and soundly.

His lips were soft but they weren't gentle. The kiss was hungry, intense and passionate. Emma had no time to think and Harry wasn't asking for permission. He wasn't asking for anything. He was demanding a response. And Emma gave him one.

She kissed him back, unreservedly. Her hormones took control, blood rushed to her abdomen, flooding her groin, and her legs turned to jelly. She knew she would have collapsed to the ground if she hadn't been in his embrace.

Eventually Harry broke away, letting her breathe, but he didn't let her go. She was shaking, panting. She wanted more. But it looked like she was going to have to wait.

'I knew you'd come for me,' she said, surprised to find she could talk and construct a coherent sentence.

'If something had happened to you, I would never have forgiven myself,' Harry replied.

'I seem to be developing a penchant for trouble.' She

smiled up at him, able to relax now she was no longer alone.

'This is a new thing for you?'

Emma nodded. 'Yes, bad luck I'm used to, trouble is something different altogether.'

'It's a good thing I'm here, then.' He looked down at her and grinned, and Emma could not disagree. There wasn't anyone else she'd rather have beside her right now.

Tony poked his head over the edge of the shaft. 'Everything all right down there?'

'Couldn't be better,' Harry answered, but his attention remained focussed on her. His bright blue gaze was fixed on her face and he was still grinning broadly.

'Shall I bring you up or do you have other plans?' Tony asked.

Emma could quite happily have stayed where she was. After being so desperate to get out of the mine, now she had to admit she was pretty comfortable.

Harry laughed. 'Let me get Emma sorted.'

She liked the sound of that.

Harry took a length of rope that was hanging from the harness and Emma saw that he had fashioned a second harness for her. He helped her to step into it and secured it around her hips. The bare skin at the tops of her thighs, where her short shorts ended, burned under his touch and her knees nearly buckled as desire flared in her groin. His kiss had her hormones working overtime. His hands were at her waist now, luckily for her as he was able to keep her upright, but the sensation of being held against him made her breathless. She could hear herself panting as she tried to breathe normally.

'Are you okay?'

She nodded. She couldn't speak.

'You're not nervous, are you? I'm going to get Tony to

take you up first and I'll be right behind you,' Harry said as he unclipped the winch from his harness and attached it to hers.

It wasn't fear that was making her breathless, it was desire. Until now she hadn't even thought about how she would physically get out of the shaft.

'You ready?'

She didn't want to go up alone. Not because she was afraid but because she didn't want to leave the sanctuary of Harry's arms. But she had no choice. She nodded and Harry called up to Tony to start winding.

As she was pulled away from Harry she hoped she hadn't had her only chance to be in his embrace. A few hours ago she'd been telling herself she and Harry could be friends, that she could control her hormones. But now she had a terrible feeling that her hormones had just hijacked her brain and she knew she'd do just about anything to convince him to satisfy the desire he'd ignited in her.

A few days ago she wouldn't have thought she'd be considering taking someone into her bed. Jeremy's behaviour had damaged not only her self-confidence but also her trust. But if she couldn't trust Harry, a man who'd just rescued her from the bowels of the earth, a man who she just happened to find extremely attractive, a man who had made her smile again, a man who had made her forget how miserable she'd been, then she doubted she'd ever be able to trust again.

Not all men were like Jeremy. She knew that. And she doubted she had enough self-control to resist the pull of attraction, to resist the flare of desire, not now that the spark had been well and truly lit. Being in Harry's embrace had reminded her that she was a woman and he was very much a man, and she was determined to see if she could get herself back in his arms.

She knew his reputation but that was of no concern, she wasn't talking about a big commitment, she wasn't thinking about anything other than a holiday fling, scratching an itch. If nearly being buried alive had taught her anything, it was that life was short. She wanted to celebrate life. She wanted to prolong this feeling of happiness. She wanted Harry and if she got the chance, she would have him. There was no place for self-control, not today.

Emma was luxuriating in a deep, hot, bubble bath at the underground motel as she examined her wounds. She had a few grazes on her hands and knees from crawling along the passage but other than that she was relatively unscathed and, she had to admit, extremely lucky.

By the time Harry had driven her back to the motel the word had spread and Denny, the motel proprietor, greeted them as if they were returning from battle. Emma's initial reaction to finding out that the entire town seemed to know of her flirtation with disaster, and of Harry's rescue, had been one of annoyance. She hated being the topic of gossip, hated having people know her business.

However, her irritation had rapidly subsided when she'd found out that her little drama had afforded her the luxury of her own bathroom. She'd been amazed to learn that the guest bedrooms didn't have private bathrooms because of the difficulty with plumbing and waste disposal in underground dwellings, and when Denny had insisted on giving her the only room with an en suite bathroom, she'd been happy to accept. That her room had an interconnecting door to Harry's was an added bonus.

She sank deeper into the bath and closed her eyes as she daydreamed about being in Harry's arms and tried to work out how she was going to get herself back there. She was planning on celebrating being alive the best way she could think of—with Harry. She just had to work out a way of getting him to agree.

'Emma? Is everything all right?'

Excellent, she thought as she heard Harry's voice at their interconnecting door. His timing was perfect.

'Denny sent me with some hors d'oeuvres and a glass of wine for you,' he called out. 'She thought it might help you relax.'

Emma appreciated the gesture but she had another form of relaxation in mind, although she wouldn't say no to a glass of wine. 'I'm still in the bath. Do you want to bring it in to me?'

'Are you decent?'

She didn't care if she wasn't but she put his mind at ease for now. She hoped there'd be time to get indecent with him later. 'I'm covered with bubbles.'

She saw the doorhandle turn and then Harry backed into the room. His denim-clad backside presented a very pleasant view. He turned round and Emma could see he had his hands full. He had two glasses and a bottle of wine in one hand and he carried a platter laden with nibbles in the other. His hair was damp, he was barefooted and his jeans and T-shirt were clean. He'd obviously had time for a shower, which was a pity as she'd vaguely entertained the idea of inviting him to share her bath. He carefully set the platter down beside the bath and once he had a hand free he poured two glasses of wine and handed one to her.

'Thank you,' she said.

'Thank Denny, it was her idea,' he replied.

'Tell me,' she said, as she helped herself to a handful of cashew nuts from the platter, 'how is it that everyone knew what had happened almost before we did?' She guessed Harry wouldn't plan on hanging around chatting while she was in the bathroom but she wanted to strike up a conversation to delay him leaving. She had another idea and needed some time to implement it.

Harry leant against the hand basin. If he felt uncomfortable chatting while she lay naked in a bath full of bubbles, he kept it well hidden. He looked happy enough to be there.

'A lot of people have their UHF radios on constantly, it keeps people connected and helps them feel less isolated out here in the middle of nowhere.'

She sipped her wine and asked, 'Don't people mind that everyone knows their business?'

Harry shook his head. 'No. I think it gives people a sense of community and a lot of them can remember the days when the only communication was through the radio, and whether you were contacting the flying doctor or doing School of the Air or chatting to a friend, everyone could listen in. People got used to having no secrets, or to choosing their words very wisely.' He grinned.

'And, quite often, it can mean the difference between life and death. If someone's in difficulty out here, the more people who know about it the more likely the problem is to get solved. It's a good thing.'

Emma hated the thought of everyone knowing her business and it was strange to think that having people so involved in each other's lives could be a good thing.

'Why does it bother you so much?' Harry asked. 'No one knows you.'

'They do now!'

'They know about you,' he said. 'That's different. You could still walk down the street and not be recognised. They won't be gossiping about you.'

Had he realised that was what was bothering her?

'It's not all about me, is that what you're saying?' she asked.

'It's not *only* about you. The mine collapse will be the

talk of the town and the airwaves for the next day or two until something else happens and then someone else will have centre stage. Is anything else bothering you?'

'Nothing that I want to talk about. In fact,' she said as she finished her wine, 'I don't want to talk at all.' She put her wine glass down and picked up the towel that was folded at the foot of the bath. If she wanted to get herself back in Harry's arms, it was now or never.

She shook the towel out and stood up, letting the towel shield her from view. She wanted to tempt him but she also wanted to test the water. If he looked horrified she would be able to back out gracefully with her pride almost intact. But she hoped he'd be tempted.

She wrapped the towel around her body and stepped out of the bath, tucking one end of the towel inside the other to keep it in place. She had Harry firmly in her sights and she was pleased to see he hadn't moved. His blue eyes were locked on her as she walked towards him and she could see his pulse flickering in his throat as he swallowed. He licked his lips as she crossed the floor.

Harry felt as though his eyes were about to pop out of his head as Emma stepped out of the bath. The towel barely covered her torso and her long brown legs glistened with water. His mouth was dry as he watched her wrap the towel around her body and tuck one end inside the other just above the swell of her breasts. All afternoon, ever since she'd been pressed against him in the mine shaft and he'd given in to temptation and kissed her, he'd been thinking about how it would feel to have her in his arms again. Having her in his arms if they were both naked would be even better.

He swallowed. His heart was racing and he felt quite light-headed—too much blood was rushing to other parts of his body and his eyes weren't the only parts of him that were popping. He could feel himself growing harder as he tried to work out what Emma was doing.

He licked his lips as she took three steps and crossed the room, stopping inches from where he stood with his back pressed against the vanity. He could see bubbles still clinging to her slim, brown shoulders and her skin was damp and shiny with moisture. She had piled her hair on top of her head but wisps had escaped and were curling around her face with the humidity of the bathroom. He could smell her now, she smelt of apples.

Her green eyes were luminous and bright and he thought again of how she would look after sex. He'd bet his last dollar she'd have the same expression in her eyes and he was determined to find out if he was right.

He stood silently, watching, taking in the vision of a semi-naked Emma. He could remember how her body had felt as she'd clung to him, long and lean and sexy as hell, and he wanted to rip that towel away from her and claim her body with his.

She was watching him watching her. She said nothing but when she smiled and her twin dimples flashed in her cheeks he couldn't resist any longer. If she was going to stand so close to him, barely dressed, she couldn't blame him for what happened next.

He hadn't wanted to let her go this afternoon and he wasn't going to let her go now.

He grabbed a fistful of fluffy white towel and dragged her to him. It was only a matter of inches before he could bend his head and claim her mouth with his.

Her lips were soft and forgiving under his. He teased them apart with his tongue and she opened her mouth willingly. She tasted of wine. Her mouth was warm and moist and he felt her arms wind around his neck.

His hands moved lower, cupping her buttocks, which were round and firm under the towel. She moaned and thrust her hips towards him and he could feel her pelvis collide with his erection. Now it was his turn to moan.

She pulled his shirt out from his jeans and slid her hands up his back. They were warm against his skin.

'What do you want, Emma?'

He had a fair idea of where this was headed but he had to hear her say the words. He had to know she wanted it as much as he did. She'd had a traumatic day and he didn't want to take advantage of her but he did want to take her. To claim her. To have her. And if she didn't object he would have her right here, right now, on the cool tiles of the bathroom floor.

Emma stepped back and let her towel drop to the floor. 'I want you to make love to me.'

Harry watched, mesmerised, as the towel fell to the floor. Automatically his eyes followed the movement as gravity took hold, and his gaze was now focussed on the towel where it lay in a pool of white around Emma's ankles. His eyes travelled upwards, up the length of her bare legs, long and tanned, to her slim hips, to the dark triangle of hair at the junction of her thighs.

He couldn't speak. A severe lack of blood to his brain had robbed him of the power of speech. But he could admire. So he did.

Emma was naked and she was gorgeous.

His gaze travelled higher, over her flat stomach and her round belly button to her small breasts and erect nipples. She was perfect.

He could see her pulse beating at the base of her throat. Her lips were parted, her mouth pink and soft, her eyes gleaming. She was dazzling.

Harry swallowed. There was only so much temptation

he could stand. He forgot about not being able to speak. He only had one thought. *Get her into bed before she comes to her senses.*

With one step he closed the gap that had opened between them and, without warning, scooped her into his arms. Her skin was warm from the bath and so soft. Inches of her bare flesh pressed against him as he held her. He could feel his erection growing larger with every passing second.

Emma wrapped her arms around his neck as he carried her to the bedroom. One, two, three, four steps across the room until he reached the bed where he gently laid her down.

He ran his fingers up her thigh, cupping the curve of her bottom. Emma closed her eyes and arched her hips, pushing herself closer to him. He bent his head and kissed her. She opened her mouth, joining them together. Harry ran his hand over her hip and across her stomach, his fingers grazing her breasts. He watched as her nipple peaked under his touch and she moaned softly and reached for him, but he wasn't done yet.

Her eyes were still closed as he pulled the clip from her hair and let it tumble around her shoulders. He pushed her hair back, exposing her breasts. He flicked his tongue over one breast, sucking it into his mouth. He supported himself on one elbow while he used his other hand in tandem with his mouth, teasing her nipples until both were taut with desire. He slid his knee between her thighs, parting them as he straddled her. His right hand stayed cupped over her left breast as he moved his mouth lower to kiss her stomach.

Her hands were on the hem of his T-shirt and he could feel her tugging at it.

'Patience, Em. Relax and enjoy,' he said, and his voice

was muffled against the soft skin of her hip bone. He took his hand from her breast and ran it up the smooth skin of the inside of her thigh. She moaned and thrust her hips towards him as her knees dropped further apart.

Harry put his head between her thighs. He put his hands under her bottom and lifted her to his mouth, supporting her there as his tongue darted inside her. She was slick and sweet and she moaned as he explored her with his tongue.

Emma thrust her hips towards him again, urging him deeper. She had one hand on the top of his head, holding him in place, not that he had plans to go anywhere. He slid his fingers inside her. She was wet and hot, her sex swollen with desire. His fingers worked in tandem with his tongue, making her pant, making her beg for more.

'Harry, please. I want you naked. I want you inside me.'

CHAPTER SIX

BUT he wasn't ready to stop. Not yet.

He knew she was close to climaxing and he wanted to bring her to orgasm like this. He wanted to taste it, to feel it.

He ignored her request as he continued to work his magic with his tongue, licking and sucking. He continued until Emma had forgotten her request, until she had forgotten everything except her own satisfaction.

'Yes, yes, oh, Harry, don't stop.'

He had no intention of stopping.

He heard her sharp little intake of breath and then she began to shudder.

'Yes. Oh, Harry.'

She buried her fingers in his hair and clamped her thighs around his shoulders as she came, shuddering and gasping, before she collapsed, relaxed and spent.

'God, you're good at that,' she said, and he could hear the smile and contentment in her voice.

'Thank you.' He lay alongside her, his hand resting on her stomach as she cuddled into him.

'Now, will you get naked?' she asked.

He turned his head to look at her. 'What did you have in mind?'

'It's your turn. And I want to feel you inside me.'

His blue eyes had changed colour. They were a dark navy now, the brightness overcome with lust and desire.

She slid one hand under his T-shirt and slipped her fingers under the waistband of his jeans. She could see he wanted to give in. 'Please?' she begged.

'Seeing as you asked so nicely,' he replied with a grin as he flicked open the button of his jeans.

This time Emma took charge. She undressed him. His boxer shorts came off with his jeans and his erection sprang free. Emma spread her legs and straddled him, trapping him between her thighs. She cupped his testes and then encircled his shaft with her hand. It was thick and hard and warm and pulsed with a life of its own as she ran her hand up its length.

Harry gasped and his body shook with lust.

'In the pocket of my jeans,' he panted, 'I have protection.'

Harry's jeans were lying on the bed beside them. Emma found a condom in the front pocket and tore open the packet. It was good to know he'd had the same plan as her, she thought as she rolled the sheath down over him.

She was sitting across his thighs and Harry's eyes darkened as she brought herself forward and raised herself up onto her knees before lowering herself onto him. Harry closed his eyes and sighed as she took his length inside her.

She lifted herself up again, and down, as Harry held onto her hips and started to time her thrusts, matching their rhythms together. Slowly at first and then gradually faster. And faster. Emma tried to stay in charge but she found it impossible to control her body. All she could think of was how good this felt and that she wanted more. And more.

'Yes. Yes.'

'Harder.'

'Oh, God, yes, that's it.'

She had no idea who was saying what, all she knew was she didn't want it to stop.

'Now. Yes. Keep going. Don't stop.'

Just when she didn't think she could stand it any longer she felt Harry shudder and she could feel his release as he came inside her. She held her breath as she let herself go and her body shook with pleasure as his orgasm was joined by hers. Their timing couldn't have been better.

They lay together looking up at the ceiling, breathing heavily as they recovered.

'So, you're not worried about people knowing your business now?' Harry asked with a gentle teasing expression in his blue eyes and a wide grin on his handsome face.

'I'm pretty sure no one is going to hear anything through these walls,' she told him. The limewashed earth walls were at least a half a metre thick and naturally soundproofed, although she knew she hadn't given it a moment's thought while she'd been caught up in the throes of ecstasy. 'I don't think any sound can get in or out of here, it's as quiet as a graveyard.'

'It wasn't a minute 'ago'. He laughed.

'I was enjoying myself,' she countered.

'I'm glad to hear it.'

A skylight was set into the ceiling, high above the bed. The sun had long since gone down and through the skylight Emma could see a sky full of stars. They were so bright, brighter than any she'd seen before, and they looked close enough to touch. She reached one hand towards the ceiling.

'It's so beautiful,' she said.

Harry turned his head and whispered in her ear. 'I couldn't agree more.'

Emma blushed, knowing he wasn't talking about the stars. He was doing wonders for her self-confidence.

He kissed her on the mouth and then sat up on the edge

of the bed. 'Why don't we get dressed? There's something I think you'd like to see.'

He stood and ducked into the bathroom, emerging with the bottle of wine and the glasses. They dressed quickly and Harry gathered two blankets and some spare pillows from the wardrobe before leading her outside. The motel was dug into the side of a hill and Harry headed for a path that led to the top. They skirted around dozens of skylights that protruded from the hill and led to the motel rooms below.

Harry stopped at the crest of the hill and spread one of the blankets on the ground. He wrapped Emma in the other blanket and pulled her down, nestling her between his thighs. The evening was chilly now, the desert ground unable to hold the heat once the sun had set, and Emma leaned back against Harry, seeking his body heat to keep her warm.

He poured them both a glass of wine and touched his glass to hers, 'Here's to new experiences.'

'Some of them I enjoyed more than others.' She laughed.

She sipped her wine, tipping her head back to look up at the sky above. It looked as though someone had thrown millions of diamonds across black silk. There was no moon so there was nothing to compete with the brightness of the stars. 'It looks like every inch of the sky has a star. I've never seen that before.'

'That's because it's a new moon tonight and there're hardly any town lights so there's no competition. The stars get their chance to shine.'

Harry was right. It was a very dark night and because most of the houses in White Cliffs were underground there were very few electric lights to be seen.

'Look over there,' he said. 'Can you see those two big,

bright stars? They're the pointer stars, Alpha and Beta Centauri.'

'What are they pointing at?' she asked.

'The Southern Cross. See those four stars?' He stretched his arm over her shoulder and Emma's gaze followed his fingers. 'Two on the long axis, two on the cross? When I see the Southern Cross, that's how I know I'm home. But I want to know what home is like for you in darkest Peru.'

'I'm not from darkest Peru.' She smiled. 'I'm from Holland Park.'

'That's in London, right?'

She nodded. It was strange to think that Harry had no concept of her life in England, strange to think she'd known him only a few days. Home already seemed like a lifetime ago. 'What do you want to know?'

'Anything you want to tell me. Do you like your job? What do you do on your days off? Have you got brothers and sisters? A dog? A cat? A boyfriend?' he asked as he topped up her glass.

'Do you think I would have made love to you if I had a boyfriend?'

'I hope not but I really have no idea.'

'No boyfriend,' Emma reassured him. 'As the Queen would say, I've had an "annus horribilis". I currently have no boyfriend, no pets, no job and no place to live.'

'That does sound pretty bad. What happened?'

'I was living with my boyfriend, my ex-boyfriend now, but I had to move my things out in a bit of a hurry when he got another girl pregnant.'

'I imagine that was awkward.'

'I guess that's one way to describe it. So I put my stuff into storage and moved back to Holland Park, into my family home, but when I go back I'll have to decide where I'm going to live.'

'What about your job?'

'I quit. Jeremy and I worked together so I decided it would be better, that *I* would be better, if I quit. So I did.'

'You worked together?'

Emma nodded. 'He's a doctor and quite a popular one too. I was quite used to people chasing after Jeremy but this one particular doctor, she was amazing to watch. She really went after him. There are always relationships happening between hospital staff, some are casual, some more serious, some exclusive, some not, but I figured, seeing as we were living together, we were in an exclusive relationship.

'I thought Jeremy was refusing Maxine's advances, because that's what he told me, but it turns out that he wasn't and now she's pregnant.'

Emma was surprised to find that the whole saga wasn't nearly as painful any more. She wasn't sure whether it was having a chance to get some distance that had changed her perspective, or whether it was Harry, or whether it was simply the fact that she'd just had mind-blowing sex and nothing could take the gloss off that right now, but something had definitely dulled the pain.

'And it's his?'

She sipped her wine and shrugged. 'He doesn't seem to think otherwise and I don't care if it is or isn't. That he thinks it could be was enough of a reason to never have anything more to do with him. They're together for now. Whether they'll stay together once the baby is born remains to be seen, but I couldn't stay working at the same hospital as the two of them. I hated knowing that everyone was gossiping and I certainly couldn't stay living with him. So I moved my stuff out and Sophie convinced me to come for a visit. So here I am.'

'How long are you staying?'

'My visa is for three months but I'm not sure if I'll stay for all that time.'

'You haven't got a return ticket booked?'

'I have, but I can change the date if I want.'

'So no firm plans, you can be spontaneous?'

'Flexible,' she corrected. 'Things work out better for me when I keep my options open. Every time I make plans something happens that throws a spanner in the works.'

'Like what?'

'Well, I guess I never really had a chance to make plans until I was a teenager. Dad was a doctor in the air force so we were always moving. I learnt not to make plans, not to get too attached to people or places, not to look too far into the future because I never knew when we'd be on the move again.

'When I finished school I had my heart set on a gap year in Australia so because I didn't know what I wanted to do for the rest of my life I took a job in a pub to make some money to buy my ticket. I kept thinking I'd earn just a little bit more and then I'd go. That was my most ambitious, if somewhat vague plan.

'But just when I'd booked my ticket the London underground bombings happened. My stepmother was in the city that day and she was right in the thick of it. She was one of the lucky ones. She survived but she had a fractured skull and burns and she was in hospital in an induced coma. I couldn't leave then. I had to help Dad with my sisters, who were still very young. But by the time my stepmother had recovered, I at least had a career path chosen. I enrolled in nurses' college. But the next time I tried to come out here my father was diagnosed with cancer.'

'Oh, Em, that sounds horrible.' Harry wrapped his arms around her and Emma drew comfort from his embrace. It was nice to feel that someone was listening, that someone understood. 'But none of those things happened because of anything you did.'

'I realise that but it's just that any time I plan something to look forward to, something goes wrong. If I don't plan things, I don't get disappointed.'

'But you made it here this time. That must have taken some planning.'

'I have Sophie to thank for that.'

'And it must have taken a little bit of planning to move in with your boyfriend.'

'Yes, and look at what a mistake that turned out to be. Although if I hadn't been so desperate to move out of the Holland Park house, I probably would have realised Jeremy wasn't the right choice for me and not have moved in with him at all.'

'Why were you desperate?'

'Dad wasn't doing so well. He was going downhill but he wanted to be at home, not in a hospital, so I moved back to Holland Park to help my stepmother nurse him, but when he died I couldn't bear to stay there. It was too much for me. Jeremy wanted me to move in with him and because I was desperate for a change of scenery and some company other than grieving family members, I said yes. I didn't really stop to think it through.'

In hindsight Emma knew that her hatred of being lonely had been the driving force behind the move. She hadn't wanted to stay in the house where her father had died and she hadn't wanted to be alone so she'd moved in with Jeremy in haste—and had repented at leisure.

'He said we'd get to spend more time together but because of our shifts we didn't see a lot more of each other. Jeremy is the type of person who craves attention and when he wasn't getting enough from me, he took the next thing that was on offer.'

'So your father died, you moved in with your boyfriend and instead of him being there to help you through a tough time he had an affair?'

'Not immediately. As far as I know, it didn't all happen at once but, yeah, he wasn't the best boyfriend.'

It was easy to talk to Harry while they were sitting in the dark. She didn't have to see him scrutinising her face. Out here in the darkness it almost seemed as though she was talking about somebody else's life.

'He wasn't sleeping with her in your bed, was he?'

'Not as far as I know.' Emma laughed. 'From what I heard, she was telling everyone about how they spent hours together in the on-call room. I didn't know which was worse, having everyone knowing that my boyfriend was sleeping around or having it happen right under everyone's noses. I couldn't stand the idea of going to work and seeing them every day so I quit and licked my wounds until Sophie convinced me to come for a visit.'

'This has all happened in the past year?'

'Pretty much. Dad died just over a year ago. I quit my job and moved out of Jeremy's five months ago.'

'What have you been doing for the past five months?'

'Nothing really. I did a little bit of agency nursing but my heart wasn't really in it. I think it was all a bit much to deal with, Dad dying and then the drama of Jeremy. Sophie recognised that I needed a break before I did and she kept insisting that I visit until I finally gave in and agreed to spend some of my inheritance on a trip out here. I think she was right.'

'Will three months be long enough to put you back together?'

'I hope so. I spent a month in Sydney when I first arrived, I've only got two months left.'

'And then what?'

Emma shrugged. 'I'll go home and look for another job. At least I know now that I want to keep nursing, although I definitely won't be going anywhere near that hospital again, certainly not while Jeremy's fiancée is still working there with her swollen, pregnant belly.'

'They're getting married?'

'Yes. I guess at least he's doing the right thing by her. Hoping he stays faithful is her problem now. Although perhaps he will. He seems to think that a doctor is a better partner for him. Do you know he actually told me that he was moving up, that nurses were okay as girlfriends but he'd never planned on settling down with one. He wanted a doctor. As far as I'm concerned, they're welcome to each other.'

'So you're not planning on moving in with any other boyfriends in the future?'

'I don't know what I'm going to do tomorrow, let alone next year or the year after. Do you have your life all planned out? Do you know what tomorrow is going to bring?'

'Hopefully tomorrow will start with the two of us in bed together.'

'My question wasn't meant to be taken literally.' She laughed.

Harry squeezed her shoulders. 'I know, but I think this is where you and I differ. I am a planner, always have been.'

'Since you were little?'

'Yes.'

Emma couldn't understand how people could be born that way. She wondered if she would have been different if her childhood had been more settled and secure. She wondered what Harry's childhood had been like. 'I suppose that's a good thing as you're a pilot. Was that something you always wanted to do?'

'It's always been something that interested me but the reason I work as a pilot is because I can't do what I really want yet.'

'And what is that?'

'Run cattle.'

Emma frowned. 'What does that mean?'

'I wanted to run our family cattle station but from when I was very young I knew that my older brother was going to get first option and unless he didn't want it, I wouldn't get a chance.'

'Is it just the two of you?'

Harry nodded.

'And he's on the station?'

'Yep.'

'But you said you can't do what you want *yet*. What's going to change?'

'I'm going to buy my own place. I just have to save enough money.'

'It sounds expensive.'

'It is. But I have a plan.'

'Of course you do,' she said with a smile. Sometimes she thought she was the only person in the entire world who *didn't* have a plan. 'Can you tell me what it is? Or is it a secret?'

'There are no secrets out here, remember? I have a deal with my next-door neighbour. When he's ready to sell his property, I have first right of refusal.'

'You're going to live on the property next door to your brother?'

'Don't sound so concerned, we won't get in each other's way. Next door is a day's drive away.'

'Oh.' She knew she still had no real concept of the size

and scale of this country. 'So how long do you have to wait to get a place of your own?'

'I'm not in a great hurry. The longer I have before Sam wants to sell out and retire, the more chance I have of saving the money. I'm a long way off still but I'll get there eventually.'

He sounded very confident and Emma envied him his goals and self-belief and conviction.

'I can't imagine settling anywhere permanently. I think that's a legacy of my nomadic air force upbringing.'

'And I can't imagine settling anywhere else,' Harry replied, as Emma's stomach rumbled noisily, interrupting the silence of the desert night.

'Are you hungry? Shall we go in for dinner?' he asked.

'No,' she said as she shook her head. 'This all feels so surreal, being out here under the stars with no one around. I don't want to see anyone else. I don't what to share tonight with anyone but you. I'd prefer it if you took me back to bed.'

'Again?'

She nodded. 'I've been in Broken Hill for four days and I could have died twice. I want to make the most of tonight.'

'I guess you haven't had the best introduction to the Outback,' he conceded.

'You can help to make up for that,' she suggested with a smile.

Harry didn't need much convincing to skip dinner in favour of going back to bed and Emma had absolutely no regrets about the decision. She spent the night getting intimately acquainted with Harry's body and his numerous scars. He'd been telling the truth when he'd said he'd broken more than his fair share of bones and had had more stitches than he could remember.

'What's this scar from?' she asked, as she kissed a thin white line that ran above his right eyebrow.

'My head got in the way of Lucas's golf club.'

'Lucas is your brother?'

Harry nodded as Emma's fingers followed a scar under his chin. 'And this one?'

'Lucas and I were racing our motorbikes. We were going much too fast and I couldn't avoid a rock. My front tyre hit the rock and I flew over the handlebars and landed on my chin and split it open.'

'Do all your scars have something to do with Lucas?'

'No,' he grinned. 'Only half. But everything was a competition between us. Who could get to the gate first on our motorbikes, who could kill the biggest snake, who could swim the furthest across the river underwater, who could kiss the most girls.'

'Didn't you ever get tired of competing with each other?'

Harry shook his head. 'It's the way we were. Still are to a degree, although our lives are quite different at the moment. Lucas is a responsible husband and father to two kids with another on the way. It's his turn to referee the contests between his own boys now. But it was mostly friendly rivalry. You said you have a sister—didn't you compete?'

'I have two sisters, half-sisters, really, and they're much younger than me. My mum died when I was two so for years it was just me and my dad. When he remarried I had competition for the first time and I have to admit I didn't really like it.'

'How do you get on with your stepmother?'

'Good now. But I was pretty horrible initially. I was fourteen when they got married and I didn't want to share my father with anyone. When my half-sister was born I was acting up so much that Dad sent me out to Australia to stay with Sophie's family for six months. That's when I got hooked on all things Australian, but I also missed my dad and the baby so when I got home again I was a model child with dreams of a gap year. I'd grown out of my rebellious teenage phase and Dad and I did things that he couldn't do with my half-sisters so I still had time with him by myself. The next time I really had any competition was as Jeremy's girlfriend and I didn't like that either.'

'I like the challenge of a good competition. Sometimes I succeed, sometimes I don't, but it's all good.'

Emma ran her fingers over a scar that bisected Harry's left shoulder. 'Was this one from a successful challenge?'

'That one hurt,' Harry admitted. 'I came off second best in a battle between me, my motorbike and a fence post.' He held up his left hand. There was a scar running through the palm of his hand. 'I had a bone pinned in my hand at the same time and I have a pin in my tibia courtesy of my horse falling on my leg and fracturing it.'

It was amazing that there was anything left of him, Emma thought as she continued her inspection, but there was more than enough to keep her satisfied well into the next morning.

CHAPTER SEVEN

THE past two weeks had flown by in a blur of activity. Sophie and her friends were a very social bunch and there always seemed to be a barbeque, a game of tennis or birthday drinks to go to, and while everyone was more than happy to include Emma in their plans she often felt as though she was living someone else's life. As if this life was on loan to her. Which she supposed in a way it was.

She'd agreed to continue working with the flying doctor service as a volunteer and she was loving that—at least that felt like it was her thing. And it didn't hurt that it meant she was able to spend a lot of time with Harry. He was easy company and a fantastic lover and many mornings Emma was surprised to find she had the strength to get out of bed. She had never had so many orgasms in her life.

And this weekend she was getting to spend time with Harry, just the two of them, alone for the next thirty-six hours. Or almost alone.

Harry had flown her to Innamincka, seven hundred kilometres north-west of Broken Hill. It was an Outback town so small Emma almost wondered why it even existed, but this weekend the population was expected to swell to a few thousand as locals and tourists flocked to town for the annual gymkhana.

Harry and Lucas were competing in an equestrian event

so she and Harry wouldn't be alone the whole time, not once his brother arrived, but Emma didn't care. She would enjoy every minute she got with Harry and being here, away from the social hub of Broken Hill, made Emma feel as though she was at least taking part in an activity that was hers, not just one she'd borrowed from Sophie.

Innamincka's official population was just over one hundred people but Emma was already getting used to flying in and out of tiny settlements and was no longer surprised when a town consisted of a couple of streets, a pub, a petrol station and a handful of houses. What did surprise her was that this tiny town had its own racecourse. She and Harry were sitting in the temporary grandstand at the racecourse, watching the children's competitions, the first of the gymkhana events, while they waited for Lucas to arrive with the horse truck. Harry was checking his watch every few minutes, obviously getting antsy about Lucas's whereabouts.

'How long until your event?' she asked.

'It's not for a couple of hours.'

'I'm sure Lucas will be here soon,' she told him. 'I'm just going to go and freshen up.'

She leant across to give Harry a kiss. She only planned to be gone a few minutes but she enjoyed kissing him so much she wanted to do it as often as possible. She left the grandstand and merged with the crowd. It was still growing and there was a line of four-wheel-drive vehicles towing camper trailers all trying to secure a good position in the campground on the banks of Cooper Creek.

She could hear music blaring from car stereos competing with the loudspeaker as various activities were announced. There were dogs barking, horses whinnying, planes and helicopters flying overhead and motorbikes dodging pedestrians.

Emma ducked and weaved her way through the crowd, dodging kids who were clutching large sticks of pink fairy floss. She could smell onions frying on barbeques and the smell made her stomach rumble. It was dusty and noisy and chaotic and Emma soaked up the atmosphere as she tried to commit the sights and sounds and smells to memory. This would probably be the only Outback gymkhana she'd ever attend and she wanted to remember it all.

On her way back from the toilets Emma detoured past one of the horse yards and a set of temporary stables. She was keen to get a look at the quality of the Outback horses.

In the distance she spotted Harry leading a horse out of a horse truck and down a ramp. His brother must have arrived while she'd been freshening up. She changed direction and headed for Harry. He was bending over, checking the horse's legs, and Emma couldn't resist giving his bottom a pat as she walked up to him.

Harry turned his head and straightened up as Emma slid her hand into the back pocket of his jeans and squeezed.

Only it wasn't Harry. This man was a little bit shorter, a little bit heavier and quite a bit surprised. But he'd walked like Harry and even now Emma could see similarities in their posture and their faces. But it wasn't Harry, not unless he was wearing contact lenses, as this man had brown eyes, not bright blue. But they looked so similar and Emma was confused for a little longer until her brain finally kicked into gear and she realised that this man must be Harry's brother.

She blushed and removed her hand from the inside of his pocket. 'Sorry, I guess you're Lucas,' she said.

'And you must be Emma,' the man said with a smile, and the similarity between him and Harry was even more apparent then.

Emma nodded and apologised again.

'Don't worry, it happens all the time.' He shrugged. 'Twins have to get used to it.'

Emma frowned, Harry hadn't told her they were twins but there was no doubting that Lucas was telling the truth. So he was the older brother who had inherited the running of the cattle station. Was it significant that Harry hadn't told her they were twins?

'Do you know where he is?' Lucas asked, interrupting her rambling thoughts, and when Emma nodded he added, 'Would you mind getting him? I could use a hand with the horses.'

'Sure. We'll be right back,' she said, and walked away.

Harry had moved out of the grandstand and was now leaning on the railing that ran around the racecourse, chatting to a group of men. He saw her approaching and waved to her to catch her attention.

'Lucas is here,' she told him. 'He's unloading the horses and said to tell you he could use a hand.'

Harry excused himself from the group and retraced Emma's footsteps. He didn't seem to think it strange that she'd bumped into Lucas and he obviously assumed, correctly, that she'd come across him somewhere between the grandstand and the toilet blocks. He took off in that direction without waiting for further information.

'You didn't tell me you were twins,' she said as she followed in his wake.

'Didn't I?'

'No.'

'Does it matter?'

'Not to me,' she replied, but she wanted to add that it obviously made a huge difference to Harry. His only brother, his older brother, was his twin—what a difference a few minutes could have made to Harry's life.

He could have had what he wanted, the cattle station.

He could be living his dream right now if it weren't for bad timing. But she kept quiet. It wasn't her business. But she was curious to see what their relationship was like. Were they close or did this dream of Harry's create friction between them? Did Lucas even know about Harry's dream?

She didn't have to wait long for some of her questions to be answered. Harry and Lucas greeted each other with big men's hugs as she stood on the sidelines, observing.

'Where're Jess and the boys?'

'Jess's still suffering pretty badly from morning sickness. She preferred to stay home.'

'You should have brought Will and Jack with you, given Jess a break.'

'Mum and Dad will lend a hand and I don't think Jess trusted me to supervise the boys. I brought Darren instead. He's going to ride in the barrel race. He's just taken Duke for a walk, you know how fidgety he gets after being in the truck. Do you ride, Emma?' Lucas asked as he handed the reins of a pretty grey horse to Harry.

'I can ride,' she answered.

'Harry didn't tell me. I could have brought a horse for you for the weekend.'

'No, no, it's fine. I haven't ridden for a while.'

Harry was looking at her quizzically and Emma knew he'd be wondering why she hadn't told him she could ride. She'd known they were spending the weekend at an equestrian event so of course he'd be thinking it was odd she hadn't mentioned her riding capabilities.

'Can I brush one of the horses down for you?' she asked, trying to divert attention from her omission. She and Harry obviously both played their cards close to their chests.

Lucas disappeared into the truck—it was massive and Emma wondered what else they had stowed in there—and Harry passed her the reins of the grey horse. 'You can take

Lady Jane,' he said as he picked up the brushes and went over to the other horse, a beautiful, glossy black stallion, the one she'd seen Lucas lead out of the truck.

'Why didn't you tell me you ride?' Harry asked as he started to brush his horse down.

'I don't ride any more.'

'Why not?'

'Riding was something I used to do with my dad. It was one of the activities that was just for us. One of the times I didn't have to share him with anybody. I haven't ridden a horse since he died.'

Emma kept her head down. If she focussed on brushing Lady Jane she was able to talk about her father but she knew if she looked at Harry she'd find it a lot more difficult. Brushing the horse was a familiar activity, one she found soothing. The smell of horses, the warmth of the mare's flank under her hand, the sound of the soft puff of air from her nostrils as she breathed relaxed her. She'd missed the horses. She missed her dad.

Harry didn't know how to comfort her. It was clear she was thinking about her father. She was avoiding eye contact with him, focussing on the horse. He hadn't suffered through anything remotely like losing a parent and she'd lost both. He didn't think he had the right words to offer. As he racked his brain, searching for some words of comfort, any words at all, Lucas reappeared from the depths of the horse truck and interrupted his thoughts.

'Do you want to walk the horses or are you going to get a spot to watch the barrel race?' he asked.

Harry glanced at Emma.

'If it's all right, I'd like to watch some events,' she replied.

'Of course it's all right. I'll take care of the horses,' Lucas said as he shooed them off.

Harry wasn't about to argue. He took Emma's hand and walked with her back to the grandstand. Heading up into the seats, he saw someone he was keen to introduce her to. He ducked into the row of seats beside a solidly built man, several years older than him, with close-cropped grey hair.

'Emma,' he said as they sat down, 'I'd like you to meet Sam Cooper.'

'From Cooper Creek Station?' Emma asked.

'Nice to meet you, Emma,' Sam said, as he shook her hand. 'My reputation precedes me, I see.'

'Only by a few days,' Harry told him. 'How have you been?'

'Can't complain. I've got a bit of indigestion from too many onions with my snag today, but other than that I'm good, real good.'

'Where's your better half?'

'Jo is selling Devonshire teas over at the Country Women's Association tent. She loves the chance to have a good gossip, you know how women are.'

Emma listened to the two men exchanging news as she thought about what Harry had told her about Sam. She knew he was the one whom Harry intended to buy out. Harry's heart was set on owning Cooper Creek Station, Sam's home, one day.

The trouble was Sam didn't look a day over sixty and appeared to be fighting fit. It might be years before he was ready to sell his property. Emma had been so certain that Harry, with his well-laid plans, would achieve his dream but now, having met Sam, she wondered if it was going to be more difficult than Harry anticipated.

The first race was about to begin and the competitors were announced over the loudspeaker. Set out in front of the stockmen were rows of barrels, spaced at regular intervals, each with a flag protruding from the top. There were sixteen riders waiting for the start of the race. Their horses were pacing in the dirt, eager to be given their heads. Sam and Harry turned their attention to the riders assembled in front of the grandstand and Harry explained the event to Emma.

'This is a flag and barrel relay. There are four teams of four riders. The first rider from each team has to collect the flags and bring them back to the second rider, who rides out and puts the flags back. The third and fourth riders repeat the moves. The team that finishes first wins.

'Can you see the first rider in the group closest to us? That's Darren, Lucas's head stockman, on his horse Duke. Jonno is the second rider in that same team, he's one of Sam's station hands.'

The starting pistol fired and Darren on Duke shot away to a good start. Darren headed for the furthest flag and pulled it from its holder as he turned for home, gathering the other three flags on his way back. He passed the flags to Jonno, who urged his horse on as he replaced the flags. One of the other teams was not far behind and they rounded the furthest barrel almost simultaneously. The whole scene looked quite chaotic to Emma, with horses and riders passing within a few inches of each other at breakneck speeds.

She held her breath as one of the horses skidded around a barrel. The horse managed to regain its balance and she thought the rider was going to stay on its back but the next thing she saw was the rider being flung to the ground right in the path of an approaching horse.

'Oh, my God.'

Emma heard the collective intake of breath from the crowd and clutched Harry's arm as the rider attempted to jump his horse over the fallen man. For a moment Emma thought he'd succeeded but then she saw one of the horse's back hooves come down, right on the man's head. And he wasn't wearing a helmet.

The crowd was mute, stunned into silence. But the silence only lasted a few seconds and in the time it took for the rider to wheel his horse round and dismount, other spectators had leapt to their feet and raced to be of assistance.

Harry was one of the first out of his seat. He jumped off the grandstand, landing safely a few feet below where they'd been sitting, and vaulted over the railings that ran around the track.

Emma was close behind him but by the time she'd got out of the grandstand and into the arena Harry had already grabbed the reins of the riderless horse and was directing the other competitors to clear the area, keep people back and call a doctor.

Emma knew that Grace was the doctor on duty. They were already here, standing by in case of emergency. Apparently there weren't too many gymkhanas or rodeos that didn't need the services of the flying doctors in some way, shape or form and now Emma understood why. What she didn't understand was why the competitors weren't wearing riding hats.

A couple of competitors were crouched beside the injured man as she approached. 'Don't move him!' she cried. They probably knew not to move him but it was better to be safe than sorry.

She knelt in the soft sand. She licked her fingers to wet them and held them under the man's nose. She could feel small exhalations. There was a depression in his skull and his eyes were closed but he was breathing. She looked over her shoulder, searching for Grace. Where was she?

Emma wasn't used to being the first medic on the scene neither was she used to trying to assist someone without any medical equipment on hand. She didn't like the feeling of helplessness that she was experiencing. She checked over her shoulder again. Harry had cleared all the horses from the arena and was on his way to her but there was still no sign of Grace. Why was she taking so long?

'What's his name?' she asked the two men who were still kneeling beside her.

'Russ.'

She held Russ's hand and started talking to him. His eyes were still closed and he didn't respond. She had no idea if he was aware of her but she needed to talk to him. She needed to do something. Anything.

In her peripheral vision she could see Harry moving towards her but then change direction. He crossed the arena. Her gaze followed him as she kept talking to Russ. Harry was going to meet Grace. Finally she was here.

In reality Emma knew it had probably only been a minute or two since the accident, it just felt like for ever.

Grace was carrying a medical kit in one hand and had a second slung over one shoulder. Jill, one of the nurses, was with her, carrying a stretcher and a third medical bag. They were trying to jog but the equipment was heavy and awkward. Harry took one bag from each of the women, lightening their loads.

Grace knelt beside Emma as Emma told her what she knew so far.

'Right pupil fixed and dilated.' Grace took over patient care and Emma was happy to hand over responsibility. Russ had a fractured skull with intracranial bleeding. It wasn't surprising but it wasn't a good situation.

Harry crouched beside her. 'What do we need to do for Mick?' he asked.

'Who's Mick?'

Harry nodded towards a stockman, who was sitting in

the dirt. 'The guy whose horse stepped on Russ. Can you take a look at him?'

Emma nodded and stood, leaving Grace and Jill to do what they could with Russ.

Mick had had a severe fright but he wasn't injured. By the time Emma got to him his vital signs were all within normal range. 'Give him a sip of brandy and get a couple of the guys to help him away from the area. It's better if he can't see Russ being treated,' she said to Harry.

Within moments Harry had organised for that to happen and Emma was able to return to see if Grace needed any assistance. She had inserted an IV line and had a cervical collar around Russ's neck and was assembling the Jordan frame around him, mindful of possible spinal injuries. Together Harry, Grace and Emma picked up the stretcher while Jill held the drip. There were plenty of offers to help but Grace wanted people who knew what they were doing.

But there was only so much they could control. The airstrip was a few minutes' drive away and Emma wondered how they were supposed to get Russ to the plane. She thought maybe they would have to carry him all the way and she knew that would be a struggle but the alternative was completely unexpected. One of the railings in the track fence had been removed and someone had backed their ute up. They loaded Russ on the stretcher into the tray of the ute and climbed in beside him for a slow, cautious drive to the airstrip.

Emma found this method of transport difficult to comprehend but it seemed to work and they managed to get Russ loaded safely into the plane for evacuation to Adelaide. She and Harry hitched a ride back to the racecourse in the ute. She squashed herself into the front seat for the return trip between the driver and Harry.

'How're you doing?' Harry asked. He had his hand on

her knee and squeezed her thigh gently. There was no room for anything more demonstrative in the close confines of the cab.

'I'm okay now but it was a bit overwhelming,' she admitted. She was looking forward to having a few quiet moments to process what had just happened but her ideas were quickly shelved when they got back to the race track.

Sam was waiting for them as they climbed out of the ute.

'The organising committee has brought the campdrafting forward,' Sam told them. 'It's the next event.'

Emma knew this was the event that Harry had entered. She frowned. 'You're not still planning on competing?' Emma asked.

'Of course I am,' he replied.

Emma couldn't believe what she was hearing. 'After everything that just happened?'

'They're not going to cancel the entire weekend. People have put too much time and effort into organising this. Accidents happen. Things go on,' Harry explained.

'But Grace and the plane have gone. What if there's another accident?' she argued.

'Relax, Em. They'll cancel the high-risks events while the flying doc is out of the picture but campdrafting is one of the safest.'

'But—'

'Sam, could you do me a favour?' Harry cut her off. 'Can you keep Emma company while I ride, explain to her how safe it is?'

'It would be my pleasure,' Sam replied.

'Go with Sam, Em, I'll be fine.' He kissed her swiftly on the lips and added, 'I'll be back before you know it.' And then he was gone, giving her no time to protest.

She was furious. She couldn't believe he was still riding. If she'd had something to throw at him she would have, maybe that would have knocked some sense into him. But it was too late. He'd disappeared and she had no option but to follow Sam back to the grandstand. What if something happened to Harry too?

CHAPTER EIGHT

EMMA'S heart was pounding as she climbed the grandstand steps. The thought of Harry being injured made her feel nauseous. She knew she'd have to watch him. It was the only way to keep her nerves under control. She tried to concentrate as Sam talked her through the event but that took some effort.

As far as she could gather, each competitor rode separately. Their performance was judged and scored out of one hundred points, with the highest scoring competitor winning. Each rider had to separate a beast from the mob of cattle and parade it in front of the judges, before driving it through a pair of gates and out of the camp. Once outside the 'camp' they needed to manoeuvre the beast around a course and then through another two narrowly spaced pegs that marked a second gate.

Her hands were shaking with nerves as the event got under way and she sat on them in an effort to stop them from twitching.

'I've never heard of campdrafting until today,' Emma admitted as the first rider completed the course without incident.

'That'd be because it's an Aussie invention,' Sam told her. 'Watch Harry to see how it's done properly. He's bloody good at it.'

Harry was waiting for the starting signal and seeing him sitting in the saddle made Emma forget her nerves. She'd always had a vision in her head of how he would look on horseback and she wasn't disappointed. He looked comfortable and confident when he was behind the controls of a plane but on horseback he looked sublime.

He urged his horse forward. He was effortless, relaxed and seemed perfectly suited to this environment. Emma appreciated the relationship between the horse and rider. She could see how the horse responded to Harry's direction and how hard it worked to separate the steer from the mob and then kept on working, cutting back and forth, to keep the steer from getting back to the mob.

She forgot that Harry wasn't wearing a helmet. She forgot that it was still a dangerous exercise because Harry made it look easy. Okay, she was probably a little biased but she was pretty impressed. Sam was right—Harry was good.

He'd driven the steer through the first set of gates and was coaxing it around the course before heading for the final gate. She could imagine him doing this for a living and she wondered how long he'd be happy to wait until he got his cattle station. Why didn't he work with Lucas? she wondered. Was there enough work for both of them? Why was it that only one could stay on the station? Harry belonged in the bush.

His thighs flexed and strained as he guided his horse and she had plenty of opportunity to admire the way his jeans moulded to his backside as he rose out of the saddle. She could close her eyes and picture how those same thighs had felt between her legs, how his powerful glutes had driven him inside her. Watching him on horseback was almost as good as foreplay. He was sensational and she could feel herself becoming aroused. She wondered

what his plans were for the rest of the afternoon. She wondered if she could convince him to sneak off somewhere
so she could make love to him.

He lifted his hat to salute the crowd as he finished and
she let herself believe he was looking directly at her. She
pulled her hands from underneath her thighs so she could
applaud him along with everyone else in the stands. He
was magnificent. And, for now, he was all hers.

Harry tried to keep focussed on the task at hand but his
attention kept wandering to the stands, where he could see
Emma sitting, watching him. He wasn't used to being distracted but even at this distance he could feel her gaze on
him and he could easily pick her out in the crowd. She was
wearing an emerald-green T-shirt that made her eyes pop
and a felt cattleman's hat that he'd given her. She'd plaited
her hair into two plaits and they fell over her shoulders
and made her look like a teenager. Each time he turned
his horse in front of the stands his eyes drifted to her, he
couldn't help it, but somehow he managed to keep the steer
from returning to the mob and get it through the last gate.

He lifted his hat to her in salute as he finished. She was
cheering and smiling. He could see her dimples flashing in her cheeks from where he was as she clapped his
performance, and even though he knew his effort wasn't
enough to give him victory today he knew he'd be going
home with a better prize tonight.

He'd known he wouldn't win but even finding out later
that he'd come second to Lucas didn't bother him—he had
Emma to console him and it was his turn to watch her now.

The gymkhana had finished for the day with no further mishaps and everyone was at the pub for a barbeque.
Harry was at the bar, ordering drinks, and Emma was sitting with Sam and his wife Jo. She was leaning forward,

talking to Jo, and she had one knee bent and had tucked her foot into her lap. He couldn't work out how she could be comfortable sitting like that, especially when she was wearing jeans and elastic-sided leather riding boots that she'd borrowed from Sophie. Her suppleness amazed him and he felt himself growing hard just thinking about the possibilities of Emma and her flexibility.

'How about that beer you owe me?'

His carnal thoughts were rudely interrupted by his brother's arrival.

'What beer?'

'The one I get for kicking your butt in campdrafting.'

Harry laughed. He had no issue with Lucas beating him. All their lives they'd been involved in friendly competition and they'd both won their fair share of contests. Lucas had been the better rider today and Harry knew that, even without the added distraction of Emma, Lucas probably would have won as he spent far more time in the saddle than Harry did these days. 'Fair enough,' he said. He held up one finger to the barman and pointed to Lucas, asking for another beer to be added to his round. 'But don't get too cocky, you only just got over the line. You'd better watch out next time.'

'Whaddaya mean?'

'You only beat me by six points. If I get some time to practise I'll kick *your* butt next time round.'

'Not if you bring Emma.'

'What?'

'I'm surprised you even finished the course. You spent more time watching her than you did watching the cattle.'

'Can't blame a man for that,' Harry said as he paid for the drinks. 'Emma's a lot more attractive.'

'Can't argue with you there,' Lucas agreed, taking a

long pull at his beer. 'Is she planning on staying around for a while? You gonna bring her out to the station?'

Harry shrugged. 'Dunno. She's only visiting for a few months so unless she gets rostered on for the station run out to you, I can't see us getting there otherwise.'

'She seems to be fitting in all right for a tourist. Maybe she'll want to stay.'

Would she? In Harry's mind Emma was only there because Australia had seemed like a good place to escape to. He didn't kid himself that she was planning on staying. This whole trip was really just a small portion of her life, a small section of the bigger picture, and he was just one little piece of the puzzle that Emma was still trying to piece together at the moment. He knew she had no firm plans for the future and that would include no firm plans to stay in Australia, but the idea that she could decide to do just that held quite an attraction. It certainly wouldn't be a bad idea. He'd heard worse.

He saw her look up and catch him watching her. She smiled at him, her dimples creasing her cheeks. What was he doing standing here talking to his brother when Emma was sitting across the room?

'Come on,' he said, picking up the drinks.

Lucas laughed, knowing exactly where Harry's mind was. 'Am I boring you?'

'Yes,' Harry retorted. 'And I have plans for tonight that don't include chewing the fat with my brother.'

But there were plenty of other people around who were also capable of thwarting his plans. He handed Emma her drink and was rewarded with her megawatt smile and flashing dimples, but before he could slide into the seat beside her Tony arrived at the table.

'Harry, I thought that was you, mate.'

Emma had been watching Harry as he waited at the bar.

He was a man of many faces—the immaculate, organised pilot, the attentive, skilful lover, the good mate—and today she was seeing yet another side to him, that of the younger brother. She couldn't decide which one she preferred.

That was a lie—the skilful lover was definitely her favourite—but there was so much more to him and she was amazed at how all his personas suited him equally well. The pilot's uniform suited his meticulous nature but he looked just as comfortable in the Outback uniform of jeans, riding boots, shirt and cattleman's hat. That suited his physical presence and ruggedness and emphasised his masculinity.

There was no denying his masculinity. Or the fact that he was a complete package. He was a man's man but he held plenty of appeal for women too. He seemed to be everybody's friend. Everyone seemed to know him and wanted to have a few words with him. People seemed to feel a similar way about Lucas too, she'd noticed.

There was something special about the Connor boys, she thought as she watched them crossing the room, but there was only one Harry. And as each new layer of his personality was revealed to her she felt herself falling a little more under his spell.

He handed her a beer and as she smiled at him in thanks she felt a hand on her shoulder. She was so engrossed in her thoughts about Harry that this unexpected touch from behind startled her.

'Emma, I'm glad to see you're still in one piece.'

She turned her head and recognised Harry's friend from the almost ill-fated trip to the White Cliffs tourist mine. 'Hello, Tony.'

'You remember me.' He sounded pleased.

'I won't forget anything about that day in a hurry,' she told him. Out of the corner of one eye she could see Harry break into a smile and she knew he was thinking about that night, just as she was. She could feel herself blushing and forced herself to continue a conversation with Tony.

She knew if she looked at Harry her feelings would be written all over her face for everyone to see and she wasn't ready for her feelings to be on public display. She'd learnt the hard way about keeping some parts of her life private.

'What's happened at the mine? Are you going to be able to open it?'

'Yes, luckily,' Tony replied, just as Sam and Jo excused themselves from the table. Tony sat himself down in the chair Sam vacated and spoke to Emma. 'It turns out the miners who were blasting that day didn't have permits. Geologists had pegged that area as unstable so they couldn't get a blasting licence but they blasted anyway. Turns out it wasn't my excavating skills that were the problem. I'm going to add some more supporting beams just to be safe but I hope to have it open properly next month. I still can't believe our luck that it wasn't worse.'

'I'm starting to think that luck has a big hand to play out here,' Emma said. 'It's a bit like living on a roulette wheel.'

'Speaking of luck, I have an update on Russ.' Sam was back at the table and everyone fell silent at his announcement as they waited for further information. 'He's in Theatre but doctors are pretty confident he'll pull through. We're passing the hat around for a collection to help him through his recovery.'

Sam passed a large tin around the table that looked as though it had been pinched from the kitchen. As the tin did the rounds and people dropped money into it Sam pulled a large handkerchief from his pocket and mopped sweat from his brow. It was warm but not hot in the pub. The overhead fans were keeping the air circulating and Emma wondered why Sam would be feeling the heat now when he'd seemed comfortable during the heat of the afternoon.

'Are you okay, Sam?'

'Just my indigestion playing up again. It's a nuisance, that's all, especially as I deliberately avoided having onions on my burger tonight.'

It sounded to Emma as though Sam was having difficulty breathing. His breaths were shallow, making his words clipped. 'Why don't you sit down next to me for a minute?' she said. 'Catch your breath.' She put her hand on his wrist, as if to encourage him to sit, but she took the opportunity to check his pulse. His skin was clammy and his pulse felt rapid. 'Where exactly are you feeling the indigestion pain?'

'Here, at the bottom of my sternum,' he said as he rubbed his chest.

'Do you have any history of heart problems?'

'No, why?'

'I think this may be angina, not indigestion,' she told him. 'Harry, is there likely to be a flying doctor medical chest in town?' Emma knew that Grace and the plane weren't back from Adelaide yet but she also knew that the flying doctor service supplied and maintained medical chests for emergency use to the Outback towns and stations. There should be one in Innamincka somewhere.

'The pub has one.'

'Can I access it?'

He nodded. 'I'll get it for you.'

'Any other health problems?' she asked Sam as Harry went in search of the chest.

Sam shook his head. 'I'm fit as a fiddle.'

'No liver problems, kidneys okay? Are you on any other medication? Any allergies?'

'Never been sick a day in my life. Other than broken bones and a dodgy appendix, of course.'

Emma raised one eyebrow. 'Of course.'

Tony offered to keep passing the tin around in Sam's place, leaving Emma to concentrate on Sam and Sam to concentrate on his symptoms. Harry came back with the chest—a heavy, bulky, contraption that looked about as old as the town—and he also had Sam's wife, Jo, in tow.

Harry unlocked the chest and proceeded to calm Jo down as Emma searched the chest for the GTN spray. She found it quickly and administered it to Sam. The spray resolved Sam's symptoms and his 'indigestion' settled within about ten minutes.

'It's not indigestion,' Emma said. 'It's your heart.'

'Is he having a heart attack?' Jo asked.

Emma shook her head. 'No, it's angina but Sam will need to see his doctor for a check-up as soon as possible,' Emma replied.

'Don't forget Sam lives on a cattle station hundreds of miles from any medical support,' Harry reminded her. 'The next doctor he sees will be Grace when she gets back here.'

It was amazing that people survived out here at all in this remote corner of the world, Emma thought. If it wasn't for luck and the flying doctor, she doubted anyone would! 'Well, you need to have some tests done,' she said to Sam and Jo.

'Can't I just get some of that spray?' Sam asked. 'That's done the trick.'

'You need to find out what's causing the angina. Some things are more serious than others. In the city I'd be booking you in for a cardiac work-up.' She turned back to Harry. 'What happens out here? Where can we refer Sam to?'

'A cardiologist visits Broken Hill once a month. Grace can refer Sam to that clinic, otherwise he'll have to wait until the cardiologist does a clinic run and the closest one would be at Thargomindah.'

'And how often is that?'

'That's run by the Queensland division of the flying doctor service but if it's anything like the specialist clinics in our region, probably once every six months.'

Emma raised both eyebrows. What she considered basic health care was certainly hard to come by out here.

'If I find out when and where the next clinic is, can you get to it?' she asked Sam.

'I'll make sure we do,' Jo replied. 'But what do we do now?'

'Are you staying in town tonight?'

'Yes. We're in our camper trailer.'

Emma paused for a minute as she tried to work out what the best course of action would be. 'What time is Grace expected back?'

'They're on their way now,' Harry said. 'ETA in the next half-hour.'

'There are a couple of sprays in the chest. Can I give one to Jo?' she asked, and when Harry nodded she handed Jo a spray and issued instructions. 'Take this with you. Sam can have it as often as needed. If he gets chest pain during the night, give it to him again and then wait five minutes. He can have more after five minutes if his symptoms haven't eased but if there's no change after three doses you'll need to get the flying doctor. Is that clear?'

Emma waited for Jo to nod before she turned back to Sam.

'How are you feeling now?'

'As good as gold.'

'No dizziness, no headache?'

He shook his head. 'Not a thing.'

'Okay, I guess you're good to go. Off to bed is the best thing for you but no strenuous activities.'

'The idea never entered my mind,' Sam replied.

'It entered my mind,' Harry whispered in Emma's ear as Sam and Jo thanked her and headed for the door. 'Are you ready to make a move?'

'Shall we walk back to the campsite with Sam and Jo?'

'We're not going to the campsite. Lucas, have you got my keys?'

Lucas tossed Harry a set of keys, which he caught in one hand.

'What are they for?' Emma asks.

'My motorbike.'

'Your motorbike?' Was there anything Harry couldn't do? He could ride horses, muster cattle, fly planes, drink beer, satisfy women *and* ride motorbikes. No wonder men wanted to be him and women wanted to be with him. 'Where are we going?'

'To a friend's property, somewhere a bit more intimate than a campsite we'd be sharing with five hundred others,' he said as he picked up their packs and they said their farewells.

Emma knew that as they left the pub she'd be getting plenty of envious glances from the women but she much preferred this to the looks of pity she'd got in England after the disastrous relationship with Jeremy.

Harry stopped beside a large dusty bike and strapped their packs and a canvas swag onto the back of the seat.

'How did Lucas get your bike here?'

'In the horse truck. There was plenty of room for a few horses, a bike and a couple of camp beds. That's where Lucas and Darren will bunk down for the night.'

'You're a self-sufficient lot, aren't you?'

'Out of necessity,' Harry said, handing her a helmet.

'But you've seen how we'll all pitch in when needed. We need to work together if we're going to survive.'

Emma knew what he meant and she could see the attraction of this rural community. While the location might be isolated, the people certainly weren't.

She swapped her hat for the helmet, pulling it onto her head and fastening the chin strap as Harry stowed their hats on the bike. She climbed up behind him and wrapped her arms around his waist as they rode out of town.

His back was warm and solid against her chest, her groin was pressed up against his pelvis and the motorbike vibrated between her thighs. She'd never ridden a motorbike before and she was finding the whole experience rather erotic.

The full moon bathed the dirt road in yellow light. The sand here was much whiter than the land around Broken Hill and in Emma's eyes it looked as though they were travelling along a beach. Eventually she felt the bike slowing and Harry turned off the road and bumped over a cattle grid as he rode onto his friend's property. He negotiated a few dips and turns for several minutes before stopping under a stand of trees and switching off the engine. The ground dropped away in front of them.

Emma jumped off the bike, not at all surprised to find her legs were a little unsteady, and walked to the edge of the little dip. She found herself looking down onto a small billabong. The water was moving with a slight rise and fall and the moonlight was dancing on the rippling surface. She wondered where the current was coming from.

'Fancy going skinny-dipping?' Harry asked.

'Are we the only ones here?'

Harry laughed as he pulled his shirt over his head, not bothering to undo the buttons, and threw it onto the bike.

'The nearest person would be fifty kilometres away; I don't think they'll happen to come past at this time of night.'

'So it's just you and me and miles and miles of empty space?' she asked as Harry stepped on the back of his boot and pulled it from his foot.

'There'll be a few animals roaming around but no people.' He took the other boot and his socks off and stuffed one boot inside the other and stood them on the ground.

Emma glanced over her shoulder into the darkness around them. 'What sort of animals?'

'Cattle mostly—although they'll be sleeping. Rabbits, dingoes, maybe some wild pigs.'

'Are we safe out here?' Her voice caught in her throat, not from fear but because Harry had stepped out of his jeans and boxers and was standing naked in front of her.

'Perfectly safe. I've been sleeping out like this since I was a kid,' he said. Turning, he stepped down the embankment and into the billabong.

His body was darkly tanned with the exception of his buttocks, which shone white in the moonlight. His bottom was tight and round and muscular and the sight of his naked cheeks as he stepped into the water made the blood rush to her groin. She felt slightly dizzy but she didn't want to sit down, not when all sorts of creatures could be climbing over her in a matter of seconds. She wanted to hold onto Harry.

He called to her from the water. 'But if you're worried, come and join me. Most of the animals don't like to get their feet wet.'

She fully intended to join him but she was going to brave the creepy-crawlies for a few minutes while she made Harry beg.

She pulled her boots and socks off first, thinking as she

did so that there was a reason women didn't wear work-boots when they were doing a striptease.

'Put one boot inside the other, like I did with mine, and throw your clothes on the bike.'

'Why?'

'It stops the bugs from getting in.'

Obviously her disrobing wasn't erotic enough to stop him from thinking about bugs! She'd need to work on that but she did as he told her, stuffing her boots and then resisting the urge to sprint to the water once her feet were bare.

She forced herself to go slowly. He wasn't begging yet but he was watching her and she enjoyed drawing out the inevitable. She undid her jeans and turned her back to Harry before she bent forward and slid her trousers down her legs. Her efforts were rewarded with a 'Hurry up, woman, I'm dying here' from Harry.

She turned back to face him. 'Patience, patience. Good things come to those who wait.'

She reached behind her back and undid her bra so she could slip her shirt and bra off together. She pulled her shirt over her head, exposing her breasts, and heard Harry catch his breath. She was almost naked.

She threw her clothes onto the motorbike and stepped out of her underwear, looping them over the handlebars. She stood, naked in the warm night air, and pulled the elastic bands from the ends of her plaits and shook her hair out around her shoulders before she joined Harry in the billabong.

'It's warm!' she said as she slid into the water and into Harry's embrace.

'It's artesian water, straight out of the ground. It's just what I need for my aching muscles.'

'What's wrong with your muscles?'

'I'm out of practice. Not enough time in the saddle.'

'Is that right?' Emma grinned. 'Let me see if I can help you with that. Where are you sore?'

'Here.' He rolled his shoulders and Emma ran her hands up over his chest to knead the muscles in his arms and shoulders.

'And here.'

He moved her hands from his shoulders to his lower back and the movement brought her closer to him. Their groins were pressed together and she could feel his erection, thick and hard, against her stomach. She rubbed the palm of her hand against the small of his back and each thrust of her hand pressed him tighter against her.

She moved her hands lower and cupped his buttocks. They were firm and spherical under her palms. She slid her fingers into the cleft between his cheeks and watched as he closed his eyes. His lips parted as he panted softly.

Emma brought one hand to his groin and cupped his testes, rolling them between her fingers before she slid her hand up the length of his shaft and ran her fingers lightly over the tip. Harry moaned and lifted her off her feet, pressing her hard against him. She wrapped her legs around him and floated effortlessly in the water, pinned firmly against him.

He bent his head to her breast and took it in his mouth. His tongue was warm as it flicked over her nipple, making it peak. He moved his mouth higher and she tipped her head back, exposing her throat as he kissed her neck before moving to her lips.

She didn't want to wait any longer. It felt like she'd been ready for this for hours, she'd been in a state of arousal since she'd watched him riding in the gymkhana. He was ready too, she could feel his erection pressing into her stomach.

She wrapped her arms more firmly around his neck

and lifted herself up, before lowering herself onto him. She heard him gasp as she took him inside her and then he took control. His hands were on her hips as he raised and lowered her, penetrating deeper with every thrust. There were no words, they didn't need words, but she cried out as Harry took her to a peak of desire, bringing her to orgasm in the warm Outback waters. She felt him climax with her as she clung to his torso, coming together until they were both spent.

CHAPTER NINE

HARRY held her hand as they floated in the water, side by side, gazing up at the heavens while they caught their breaths. Even with the full moon Emma could still see a million stars.

'I feel like I'm in a parallel universe,' she said when she found her voice. 'It's magical out here, isn't it?'

'This is why I can never leave. I'm a part of this land, it's in my soul and in my blood.'

Emma knew why he would feel that way, she was starting to understand how hard it was going to be to leave here herself after only a few weeks. 'I think I know what you mean. This land is special. I don't feel it when I'm in town but when I'm out here under the stars I feel at peace.'

'I was hoping you'd feel a connection. This land is good for your spirit. If you can let go and relax, it will help to heal you.'

Emma laughed. 'If I was any more relaxed now, I'd drown.'

'Do you think you can be trusted not to drown while I get out and make a fire?'

'I'll do my best.'

Emma floated on her back and listened to Harry gathering sticks for the fire. She turned her head and watched as he set up their camp. He was focussed on his tasks and it was a good chance to ask the question that had been bothering her all afternoon.

'Why didn't you tell me you and Lucas were twins?'

'Why didn't you tell me you could ride?'

'That's not the same thing and you know it,' she protested. 'Riding never came up in conversation, Lucas did, and the way you talked about him made it sound as though he was years older than you, not minutes. It doesn't seem fair that he gets the station because of a few minutes.'

Harry put a billy of water onto the camp fire to boil. 'Twins or not, he's still the oldest son.'

'Does he know about your dream?'

'He knows. But what can he do? If he hadn't wanted to run the station, it would have come to me, but he does. And he should have it.'

'Why can't you both live there? Is it big enough for two of you?'

'It's plenty big enough,' he said as he unrolled the canvas swag and pulled a blanket out before rolling the swag back up again to use as a seat. 'But that never works. It only needs one chief and I don't want to be an Indian. My parents are still on the property too.' She'd forgotten that fact. 'That's too many Connors,' Harry continued. 'I think Lucas's wife might draw the line at having me there as well.'

The billy was boiling as she emerged from the billabong. The night air was cool after the heat of the water and Harry wrapped the blanket around her naked shoulders and sat her on the swag. He poured her a mug of tea and served it with biscuits as he finished explaining.

'I knew from an early age that I'd have to make my own way. I get an income from the station but I don't get to run it and that's what I really want. The trouble was Lucas wanted it too. So it's up to me to make my own future. And that's okay. One day I'll have what I want. I'm not going to

let a matter of a few minutes ruin the relationship I have
with Lucas. That's more important than anything else.'

She couldn't argue with that. She knew from experience that having a family was far more important than
having a place to live. From her nomadic childhood years,
when her father had been the only constant in her life, she
knew how important family was. Harry was lucky to have
such a strong relationship with his brother and she knew
he wasn't the type of person to jeopardise that. He valued
his friends and family far too much. And if he was okay
with the situation, it wasn't her place to judge.

As she finished her tea Harry unrolled the swag beside the fire and they lay together on a sandy bed under
the Southern Cross.

'Do we have to go back tomorrow?' Emma asked.

'I guess you don't, but I do. I'm expected at work on
Monday.' He slid one arm underneath her shoulders, hugging her into his side. 'You know, you could always make
some enquiries about extending your stay.'

'Make plans to stay longer?'

'Why not? There's nothing waiting for you at home that
couldn't wait a bit longer, is there?'

Home. It seemed such an alien concept at the moment.
Her old life seemed so long ago. But Harry was right, there
was nothing waiting for her at home. 'I guess I could…'
But staying longer would mean making plans, making a
commitment, and she wasn't sure she was ready for that
either.

'But? There's a but in there, isn't there?'

She nodded. 'But I don't know if it's what I want. And
that's the trouble. I don't have any idea about what I want
to do with my life. I need a passion.'

She tried to explain her feelings but it was difficult
when she didn't understand them herself. The longer she

spent in the Outback the more confused she was getting about what she did and didn't want. While she loved aspects of the life here, there were other parts—the dust, the flies, the remoteness—that she didn't know if she'd ever get used to.

'I envy you. You have your flying and your dreams. I know one day you'll achieve your goals. I'm still trying to work out what mine are.'

'Well, that's what you should use this time for. You're away from your old life, away from all the old expectations. Take some time to figure out what floats your boat. All I'm suggesting is that if you're not ready to go home in a few weeks, you could probably stay a bit longer.'

But that would take planning—she didn't imagine she'd be able to decide on her last day that she wasn't ready to leave and be able to stay. It was more than likely that she'd have to start thinking about it now and that was too daunting. Anything could happen in the next five weeks.

It was all too much to think about—what would be the point of making enquiries if she didn't know what she might want to do?

'So, tell me all about last night,' Sophie said as she lay across the foot of Emma's bed, desperately waiting to hear all the details.

Emma was exhilarated but exhausted. The past thirty-six hours had been non-stop and she was longing to put her head on her pillow and catch up on some sleep, but she knew she'd have to tell Sophie something. The trouble was she didn't know where to start, she wanted to keep parts of last night to herself. Some parts were not for sharing.

She could tell her about Russ's accident, about Sam's angina attack, about meeting Lucas, about sharing billy tea and toast by the campfire with Harry this morning before they'd ridden back into Innamincka, but she knew that wasn't what Sophie wanted to hear.

'I bet you weren't thinking about Jeremy.'

'Who?' she asked with a smile. 'I've barely thought about Jeremy since I got here.' She actually hadn't thought about him at all for the past two weeks, her head had been too full with thoughts of Harry.

Sophie laughed. 'Harry's been a good distraction, then?'

Emma grinned. 'You could say that.'

'I knew this trip would be the perfect pick-me-up for you. So, what are your plans?'

'No plans. You know me. Are you trying to get rid of me?'

'No, you're welcome to stay as long as you like. I love having you here and I know Grace doesn't mind having you in the house. It's easy with the spare room.'

'I'm sure you don't want me freeloading with you for ever. I'll stay until my visa expires. I've got five weeks left.'

'You could always get a real job and stay longer.'

'Not on a tourist visa I can't.'

'You're half-Australian, you could always ask. Wouldn't they have to let you stay?'

'I have no idea. They'd probably deport me.'

'I'm sure the flying doctor service would sponsor you. And what will you do when you get home? Where will you live? Where will you work?'

She had nowhere to go, nothing to go back for. First Harry and now Sophie had implied as much and she knew they were right. But England was her home. She couldn't stay here indefinitely.

'I don't know. Something will come up. It always does.' What would it be like to stay here? 'I'm not sure that this is the place for me. I've been here three weeks and I've survived a plane crash, being buried alive and seen other people sustain injuries I never imagined seeing. I'm not sure I'm cut out for Outback life.'

'Not even with the perks?'

Emma knew what, or who, Sophie was referring to. 'Not even then. You told me yourself he has a reputation as a ladies' man. That there are a string of broken-hearted women scattered across the country. It's a nice interlude but it's just a holiday fling. That's not a good enough reason to pack up my life and move halfway around the world.' She wondered if she sounded convincing.

'Your mother did it.'

'She wanted to marry my father. One of them had to move.' That wasn't the same thing at all.

'It started as a holiday romance, didn't it? What if you're not so different from your mum?'

'You're forgetting one thing,' Emma said. 'They were in love.'

Maybe she and her mum had more in common than just their looks. She knew she could easily fall in love with Harry, it was hard not to feel smitten by him, he was as close to perfect as it was possible to be, but she wasn't about to admit that to Sophie. She wasn't about to admit that to anyone. As far as she, and everyone else, was concerned, this was purely and simply a holiday fling. And it would come to an end sooner rather than later.

'I promise I'll come and visit again,' she said to placate her cousin. She knew that wasn't the same thing as living here permanently, but surely that was out of the question?

It was one of the quieter days Emma had had at the flying doctor base but years of working in hospital emergency departments meant that she knew better than to say so. Old superstitions existed through the ages for a reason.

She and Grace were sitting together, sorting supplies

and bundling medications to restock the emergency medical chests for the stations; it was simple work that involved cross-checking the requests with the records, showing what had been used and marking off the items as they were gathered. It didn't require huge concentration, not with two of them working, and Emma's thoughts drifted to the myriad discussions she'd had with Sophie over the past week. Her cousin had been like a dog with a bone, trying to convince her to stay in Australia.

In fact, she'd been bugging her so much that to keep the peace Emma had actually made some enquiries. As she'd suspected, she couldn't apply for a working visa while she was in the country on a tourist visa, but what had surprised her was that she also had to leave the country to apply for Australian citizenship.

She knew why she'd given in and made enquiries in the first place and she also knew her reasons were not that sensible. She wasn't ready to go home because she wasn't ready to leave Harry but that wasn't a good enough reason to stay so it was a relief to have an excuse not to take it any further. The more difficult it was, the more reason she had not to pursue it. It wasn't as if she had a good reason to stay.

She and Harry were nothing serious. It was just a holiday fling and just because she wasn't ready for it to be over it didn't make it a reason to move to the other side of the world. Sure, her mother had done it, as Sophie had pointed out, but she had been in love. It was a completely different situation.

Emma's gaze drifted away from the medications and across the room to Harry. He was sitting at another table, writing something in a logbook, but whenever he was nearby Emma was aware of his presence, and the more time they spent together the more aware of him she became. She knew her feelings about Harry were influencing her actions as much as anything.

Harry looked up from his paperwork and saw her watching him. He winked at her and smiled and her heart skipped a beat, just as it did whenever she had his undivided attention.

But just because her heart skipped a beat whenever he touched her, just because he made her happy, just because their sex life was amazing and just because she didn't want it to end, it didn't mean she should stay. No, her relationship with Harry wasn't the same thing as her parents' relationship at all. She wasn't her mother and she couldn't move to the other side of the world because of a man.

Not even when her heart was telling her that Harry wasn't just any man?

No. She shook her head, mentally admonishing herself. It was a ridiculous idea to entertain. She didn't have a job, she didn't have a visa and she wasn't making plans around men again, especially when the man in question hadn't even asked her to stay.

No, this whole thing was all Sophie's idea and Emma decided she'd be better off putting it right out of her mind. She wasn't going down that path.

'Can I see you in my office, Emma? I need to speak to you.'

Irene stuck her head into the common room and interrupted Emma as she was focussed on counting bandages and trying not to think of Harry. She made a note of where she was up to and pushed her chair back from the table. She felt Harry watching her and she could see the question in his eyes, but she had no idea why Irene needed to speak to her. She shrugged and followed Irene from the room.

Emma was surprised and a little stunned by the conversation that followed but when she returned to the common room she was still aware enough of her surroundings to notice that Harry was still poring over his logbook and Grace was on the phone, obviously dealing with an incident. Harry looked up but before they could speak Grace interrupted.

'Harry, this call, it's Jess,' she said.

'What is it?'

'She's had a fall. Off a ladder.'

Emma thought Grace must be talking about Lucas's wife. Her name was Jess and that would make her Harry's sister-in-law, Harry's *pregnant* sister-in-law.

'What the hell was she doing up a ladder?' Harry's voice was brusque and Emma knew that wasn't the question he'd meant to ask but worry made people ask unexpected things. She knew she'd ask the same irrelevant question in his shoes.

'I didn't ask,' Grace replied.

'How bad is it?' Emma jumped in. That was what they really needed to know and she hoped it was something Grace could answer.

'She's conscious and she doesn't think she's broken anything but she's complaining of abdominal pain,' Grace replied.

'The baby?' Harry asked and Emma could hear the catch in his throat, the concern in his voice.

'She's not bleeding,' Grace told him, 'but she hasn't felt the baby move since the fall.'

'How long?'

Grace glanced at her notes and then at the clock on the wall. 'Fifteen minutes. I told Lucas we're leaving now.'

Harry was already standing. Emma hadn't yet sat down.

Grace put her hand out, stopping Harry as he was about to race past her. 'Are you okay to fly? Do you want me to call someone else in?'

'I'm fine.' Harry shook her hand off. 'We're wasting time.'

Emma and Grace exchanged glances. The other crew was down at Menindee; Emma knew it would be quicker to get to Connor's Corner from the base but they couldn't afford Harry to be distracted. Grace nodded at Emma and she relaxed; if Grace thought Harry wasn't up to it, she'd stop him. They grabbed what they needed and hurried to the plane.

Harry hadn't waited for them. He was already in the pilot's seat and he'd dumped his logbook and cap on the co-pilot's seat. Emma had got into the habit of sitting next to him when they had no patients but today he was sending a pretty clear message that he wanted to be alone.

His message hurt but Emma said nothing. What could she say? Harry was clearly preoccupied and concerned and if he wanted space she had to give it to him, but it stung to be shut out like this.

Emma took the seat in front of Grace. Grace attempted to start a conversation but soon gave up when Emma's responses were less than enthusiastic. Emma felt bad but she had a lot to think about and she wasn't in the mood for talking.

The two hours spent in flight were two of the longest hours of Emma's life, right up there with when she'd sat beside her father's bed and watched him succumb to cancer. She felt as helpless now as she had then. Normally, racing to the rescue made her feel useful, important even, but today she realised for the first time that, even with the flying doctors, people were still a long way from help in an emergency.

Emma felt the plane begin to lose altitude and she swivelled her seat to look out of the window. The land beneath them was streaked with green and red and to the north-east a muddy green ribbon of water wound its way across the earth.

Grace had turned to look out of the window too and this time when she spoke Emma was ready to listen.

'We're almost there. That's Cooper Creek,' Grace said as she pointed at the muddy green river. 'Can you see where it turns the corner, that almost ninety-degree bend? That's the south-eastern corner of the Connors' station, that's where the station got its name. The river turns west there and heads to Innamincka.'

Emma had been keen to see Connor's Corner but not this way. Not on an emergency flight to treat one of Harry's family.

'On the other side of the creek is Cooper Creek Station, Sam's place,' Grace said, giving Emma her bearings.

Emma watched out of the window as the plane followed the course of the river before banking left and flying over the homestead. She could see dozens of buildings, sheds and several houses plus cattle yards. It looked like a small town and not at all what she'd expected. How many people lived there?

Harry touched down smoothly on the dirt airstrip and taxied off the edge of the runway, stopping next to a four-wheel drive that was being driven by Harry and Lucas's dad, Andrew. Emma had forgotten that Harry's parents lived on the station too. It seemed everyone lived there except Harry.

Andrew was an older, heavier, shorter version of Harry and Lucas but he had the same bright blue eyes as his younger son.

Emma and Grace gathered the medical kits as Harry embraced his dad.

'How's she doing?' Harry asked.

'I don't know. Your mother won't let me near them.

Lucas is in there, the boys are with the governess. The only thing they think I can handle is meeting the plane.'

With Andrew's help they loaded their gear into the vehicle as Harry very quickly introduced Emma to his father before jumping into the front seat and continuing his questions.

'What was she doing up the ladder? Why didn't she ask for help?'

'Lucas and I were out in the machine shed. Jess wanted to get some baby clothes down from storage and she couldn't wait—you know what women are like,' he said as he pulled the car to a stop in front of a large house.

Lucas had heard them arrive and was standing on the wide veranda of a single-level house at the top of a short flight of steps. Andrew had barely switched the engine off before Grace grabbed the medical bags and leapt from the car. Emma hoisted the portable ultrasound machine from the boot and followed at a run across the lawn that separated the house from the dust.

Lucas nodded briefly before he turned and led the women into the house.

Jess was lying on a single bed in the boys' room. She had her knees drawn up in a protective posture and a sheen of sweat glistened across her forehead. An older woman Emma assumed was Harry's mum sat beside Jess. She had a damp facecloth in her hand and had obviously been wiping Jess's face. An overturned ladder lay by a wardrobe and baby clothes and linen were strewn across the carpet beneath an open overhead cupboard door.

'Lucas, can you see if you can calm Harry down? He's a bit jumpy. Leave Jess to us,' Grace said, coming up with a reason to shoo Lucas from the room. There were enough people in here already.

Emma pulled the sphygmomanometer from the bag

and started to take Jess's obs as Grace introduced her to the other women.

'How are you feeling, Jess? What's happening now?'

Jess put one hand over her stomach, just left of her belly button between her ribs and hip. 'I've got pain here.'

Grace lifted up Jess's shirt. Her abdomen was rounded with the pregnancy but there were no obvious bruises or marks to be seen.

'How did you land?'

'I fell sideways but I caught my back on the edge of Jack's bed.'

Harry's mother, Melissa, reached down to the floor and lifted up a bedpan. 'Jess needed the toilet, I thought you might need to see this,' she said as she held the pan out towards Grace. Emma could see urine in the pan but it was streaked with blood. Dark red blood. In sufficient quantities to be alarming.

'Can you roll onto your right side for me?' Grace instructed, and somehow Jess managed to comply.

There was a bruise already starting to show on the left of Jess's lower back.

'Blood pressure normal, heart rate a little elevated,' Emma reported.

'Have you felt the baby move since you called us?'

Jess shook her head.

Over two hours.

Emma hoped the baby had been moving and that Jess hadn't felt it because she'd had her mind on other things. Like pain. She moved the stethoscope onto Jess's tummy, listening for the baby's heartbeat.

'You're twenty weeks?' Grace confirmed. 'You've felt the baby move before?'

Jess nodded.

'Third pregnancy,' Melissa said. 'Everything happens earlier.'

'Got it.' Emma found the baby's heartbeat and made sure she told Jess immediately, assuming Jess would be thinking the worst. 'It's good and strong.' Emma looked at her watch as she timed the beats. 'One-twenty.' It was possibly a little slow but otherwise seemed okay.

'The baby's okay?' Jess's eyes welled with tears.

'As far as I can tell,' Emma said.

'I'll do an ultrasound to double-check. It's not as sophisticated as the ones you get in the hospitals but it might be useful,' Grace said as she palpated Jess's back.

'Where's the...' Harry's mother paused and glanced down at the floor where she'd put the bedpan '...pain coming from, then?'

Emma knew she'd been about to say blood before she'd stopped herself. She couldn't have told Jess that there was blood in her urine.

Emma was monitoring the baby's heartbeat while Grace checked Jess's ribs and spine, but Grace looked up when Melissa paused and Emma saw her register the comment.

Jess gasped as Grace's fingers pressed over her left kidney.

'I think you might have bruised a kidney,' Grace told her. 'That would fit with the mechanics of the fall and your symptoms,' she said as she nodded at Melissa.

'What do we do?'

Grace addressed Jess. 'Jess, there was some blood in your urine. It's more than likely to be from your kidneys. I'm pretty sure it's not from the baby, but I'm going to do the ultrasound just to check.'

Emma was setting up the portable ultrasound when there was a brief knock on the door and Harry stuck his head into the room.

'Grace, how are you going here? The base is on the radio, they need us over at Cooper Creek Station if it's at all possible.'

'What's happened?'

'It's Sam. He has chest pain that's not settling. Jo thinks it might be a heart attack.'

CHAPTER TEN

'EMMA, can you go to the radio and speak to Cooper Creek? Find out what's going on,' Grace said as she squeezed transducer gel onto the ultrasound head and prepared to scan Jess's abdomen. 'If we need to, I think we'll be able to get to Sam from here. I'm almost done.'

Emma didn't have the slightest idea of how to use the radio. It wasn't something she'd done before but Grace had already turned back to Jess and Emma couldn't bring herself to argue. To think that just a few hours ago she'd been thinking how quiet the day was.

Harry was waiting in the doorway. He picked up on her hesitation. 'Come, I'll operate the radio for you,' he said. 'You just need to ask the questions.'

Emma followed him out of the bedroom but they only got as far as the passage before she literally bumped into Lucas. Emma couldn't believe the difference in him. He looked ten years older than Harry; worry lines had etched themselves deep into his forehead and his eyes were flat and unfathomable.

'How's Jess? And the baby?' he asked.

He'd obviously been hovering outside the door, desperate for news, and Emma couldn't blame him. 'They're going to be okay,' she told him. 'We think Jess has a bruised kidney and Grace is doing an ultrasound on the baby now, but I've heard the heartbeat myself.'

Lucas visibly relaxed as Emma's words sank in but she had no time to tell him anything more, even if there'd been more to tell, as Harry had her by one hand and was pulling her away from the bedrooms.

He led her into a study and picked up the handset for the radio.

'Push this button in to talk, and when you've finished just say "Over" and then let the button go. I'll take notes for you—just get whatever details you need.

'Jo, are you there?' Harry spoke into the handset. 'I've got Emma with me, over.'

He passed the handset to her as Jo responded and when it was her turn to talk Emma pushed the button in as Harry had shown her. 'Can you describe Sam's symptoms to me, Jo? Over.'

'He's been complaining of chest pain on and off all day but it has settled with the spray. Until now. Over.'

'How many doses of the spray has he had?'

'Three lots over the past twenty minutes but the pain isn't going away.'

'Where is the pain?'

'Behind his breastbone.'

'Does he have any other symptoms? Is the pain radiating away from his chest? Is he short of breath?'

'The pain is only in his chest but he's a bit out of breath.'

'Has he been doing any strenuous activity today?'

'No. Less than normal even. He hasn't felt well enough.'

'Okay. Make sure he stays lying down and continue to give him the spray every five minutes. We're on our way from Connor's Corner. We'll be with you in...' Emma glanced up at Harry. She had no idea how long they'd be. Harry held up three fingers on one hand and made a fist with the other. 'Thirty minutes,' she said, and was pleased to see Harry confirm that with a nod as he reached out and took the handset from her.

'Jo, can you ask Jonno to organise lighting the airstrip? It's getting dark. Over.'

'Will do, Harry. Over.'

'Stay in touch on the radio, okay? Over and out.'

Emma's hands were shaking as she pushed the chair back from the desk and stood up. The chair wobbled as she pushed it back in.

'You okay?' Harry asked, seeing the tremor in her hands. 'You did well.' He rubbed her back. 'Is it serious?'

Emma nodded as Harry continued to rub her back.

'Let's hope we get to him in time, then,' he said.

Harry's praise made Emma feel more confident but she was still concerned. 'I'm pretty sure Grace will want to take Jess back to Broken Hill—do you think we'll be able to get to Sam as well?'

'Sam's not far away. We can get him first and come back for Jess if we need to. Let's see what Grace wants to do.'

Emma still wasn't used to the idea that a thirty-minute trip wasn't considered far out here. She hoped for Sam's sake that Harry was right.

Grace was packing the ultrasound away as they came into the room. She looked up. 'Heart attack?' she asked.

Emma nodded. 'He needs attention now. How is Jess doing?'

'I want to take her to Broken Hill for observation and complete bed rest—there's not much chance of that here,' she explained. 'But there's no urgency. Jess can handle the scenic route via Cooper Creek Station. The baby seems to be sleeping and treatment for the bruised kidney is simply bed rest until the bleeding resolves. We'll take them both back to the Hill together.'

Twenty-five minutes later they had successfully transferred Jess to the plane and were landing on Sam's airstrip. Twenty minutes after that they were bound for Broken Hill with their two patients. There was no time for Emma to think about anything other than Jess and Sam as she and Grace were kept busy monitoring their charges.

Jess had a drip in place and a foetal heart-rate monitor strapped around her abdomen. Sam was attached to the portable ECG, oxygen and IV fluids. The back of the plane was full and there had been no room for Lucas or Jo to accompany their respective spouses. They would have to make their own way to Broken Hill tomorrow.

By the time Sam and Jess were safely transferred to waiting ambulances for the trip to the hospital Emma was exhausted. After a slow start to the day it was now way past their scheduled finishing time and she was looking forward to going home and putting her feet up, preferably snuggled against Harry on the couch.

'Did you want to come back to my place?' she asked him. 'I'll make us something to eat.'

To her surprise, Harry shook his head. 'Thanks, but I won't. Once I get the plane put away for the night I'm going to head to the hospital. Lucas and Jo won't be down until tomorrow so I want to be there for Jess and Sam overnight.'

Emma had never assumed she was Harry's first priority but it still hurt to know that she was right. She wished she knew where she did fit into his list of priorities. But he hadn't told her and she wouldn't ask.

She couldn't be upset with him for staying at the hospital, of course he'd choose to take responsibility for his brother's family, she would have been shocked if he hadn't. His sense of loyalty to both his friends and family was one of the things she loved about him. She loved his confidence and she loved the way she felt around him.

He made the world seem a better place, a happier place, as though it was full of good things. She loved his laugh and his ruggedness. And she loved the way he treated her, the way he had of making her feel as if she belonged here. But she didn't belong and he hadn't asked her to stay.

She couldn't believe she'd been considering accepting the job offer because of a holiday romance. Even though she knew it was more than that—for her anyway. She'd never become so quickly and completely besotted by someone. If she'd thought that Jeremy had trampled on her heart, she'd been mistaken. Sure, the experience had left her homeless, unemployed and single, but all that had really been wounded in that experience had been her pride.

She had an ominous feeling that she was going to lose a lot more than that when she left Harry behind. But she needed a better reason to stay. The trouble was, she couldn't think of one.

Emma was awake early the next day and filled the morning with odd jobs, pretending she wasn't waiting for Harry to call. Eventually she decided to visit the hospital to see Sam and Jess, telling herself she wasn't looking for Harry, telling herself she was visiting Jess and Sam because she wanted to, and in an effort to convince herself she went to the coronary care unit and sought Sam out first, knowing that Harry would more than likely be keeping Jess company.

But she couldn't quell the disappointment that rose in her when she walked into Jess's ward and found it empty of all but the patients. Harry was nowhere to be seen.

She paused in the doorway, looking at each bed, looking for Jess but also looking for Harry.

'Emma?' Jess was in a bed to her left and Emma forced

herself to bite back her disappointment and leave the doorway. After all, wasn't Jess the person she'd come to see?

'I thought that was you,' Jess said. 'Sorry, I was a bit out of it yesterday. I was in agony, not even my labours were that painful.'

'Is it better today? What have the doctors said?' Emma made an effort to ask the right questions, to avoid asking Jess if she knew Harry's whereabouts.

'I'm much better. Grace was right—bed rest is all that's prescribed. That and a few mild painkillers but I've tried not to have them. There's less blood already and the doctors think I'll be able to go home tomorrow.'

'And the baby?'

'She's fine. They've done some more comprehensive scans and everything is good.'

'She?'

Jess was grinning. 'According to the scans, it's a girl. Lucas will be stoked. I can't wait to tell him.'

'He's coming to town today, isn't he?'

'Yes. He's bringing Jo down with him. They should be here after lunch. Do you know how Sam's doing?'

'I've just been to see him,' Emma told her. 'He's comfortable but he's going to be sent down to Adelaide for more tests with the next available flying doctor run.'

Emma stayed to chat to Jess for a few minutes, killing time and hoping that Harry would return, but when Jess began to stifle a yawn Emma knew it was time to let her rest. Walking out of the ward, she ran into Harry. He must have been home at some stage as he had changed out of his flight overalls into jeans and a T-shirt that hugged his chest and biceps and made Emma want to wrap herself around him.

'Hi.' A smile lit up his face. He looked genuinely pleased to see her and he greeted her with a kiss. He was behaving as if everything was normal and Emma realised that from his perspective it was.

It wasn't his fault that she felt left out. It wasn't his fault that she wanted to be higher up his list of priorities or that she wanted to be more than a holiday fling. It wasn't his fault that she'd fallen in love with him.

Oh, that wasn't supposed to happen. She wasn't supposed to fall in love with him. This was supposed to be a holiday romance. She was supposed to be putting herself back together, not complicating her life. But that's just what she'd done. Once again her life seemed to have a mind of its own. Falling in love with someone who was expecting a short-term fling was only going to lead to complications. How was she going to fix this?

'Have you been to see Jess?' he asked.

'And Sam,' she said. 'I'm just on my way home again.' She waited for him to say he'd come with her or to ask her to hang around and keep him company, but he just nodded.

She took a step away. And another, and she was several steps from him when she heard him say her name.

'Emma, wait.'

She turned around expectantly.

'I forgot to ask you what Irene wanted to talk to you about yesterday.'

It wasn't what she'd been hoping to hear him say but she supposed it was to be expected. Today looked like being one disappointment after another. 'She offered me a job.'

'Really!' Harry's answering smile was all she needed to lift her spirits. His blue eyes sparkled and he closed the gap between them and wrapped her in his arms. She was just where she wanted to be. 'Congratulations. When do you start?'

'I don't know if I'm going to take it.'

'Don't you want to stay?' She could hear the frown in his voice.

'I don't know really. It feels a bit surreal.' As did this conversation. Standing in the middle of a hospital corridor wasn't where she'd imagined having this discussion.

'What do you mean?'

'It's not real life, is it?'

'It is for some of us.'

She could hear the wounded tone in his voice. She hadn't meant to make it sound as if there were more important things to do or better places to be. That wasn't what she thought or how she felt.

'But not for me. This is a fantasy world for me.' She tried to explain. 'It's something Sophie and I talked about as kids. I never thought I'd actually be here, let alone that I'd stay.'

'Sophie's doing it, you could too.'

'But Sophie hasn't had to move halfway around the world and she's only here temporarily. She'll move back to Sydney eventually. It's a much bigger commitment for me.'

'When do you have to give Irene an answer?'

'Soon, I guess. My visa runs out in three weeks, I'd have to make a decision by then.'

'But you don't have to decide today,' Harry said. 'Have you spoken to Sophie?'

'I haven't seen her. I was exhausted last night and she's at work today,' Emma explained, but she didn't need to discuss the job offer with Sophie, she knew exactly what she'd say.

'I want to wait here for Lucas but when he arrives I'll come past your place and if you think it will help I'm happy to be your sounding board.'

Emma realised she'd hoped he'd tell her she *had* to stay. That he wanted her to stay. And she was annoyed when he didn't. But why would he tell her that? It would make no difference to him. It wasn't his life. It wasn't his decision. And it wasn't as if he'd fallen in love with her. His response was just another disappointment to add to her list for the day.

She was tempted to say she was busy, that she couldn't sit around and wait for him, that she didn't need a sounding board, but she'd already told him she was going home and she knew saying anything else would make her sound petty and ridiculous. Besides, she wanted to see him, it was really why she'd come to the hospital in the first place, so telling him not to bother would only punish her. She went home and waited.

She didn't have to wait long. Harry came to collect her, instructed her to change into jeans and borrow Sophie's riding boots and drove her to some stables on the edge of town. He led her to the saddling yard where two horses were standing, waiting for riders.

'We're not going riding?' He knew she hadn't been riding in months, not since her dad had died. In actual fact she hadn't ridden for over a year as her dad had been too sick to go with her.

'I saw what you were like with our horses in Innamincka. You said you hadn't been riding because you haven't had anyone to ride with. I'm offering my services,' he replied. 'You need some thinking time. This is the perfect way to clear your head, to give you a chance to get some perspective.'

Emma reached out a hand and let the horse sniff her before she rubbed its neck. It was warm and soft and the familiar scent was comforting. Harry had done this for her.

Tears welled in her eyes. She'd been grumpy and thinking mean thoughts when he'd been busy thinking of ways to help her. He might not be in love with her but he'd only ever tried to do the right thing by her. He'd only ever tried to take care of her. She added that to the list of things she loved about him.

Harry rubbed her back as she rubbed the horse. 'I'm here. All you need to do is come with me. You know I'll look after you.'

The horse whinnied softly and nudged her. She didn't need to go riding but she wanted to. Badly.

Emma put aside her bad mood. She knew Harry meant every word. He wouldn't deliberately hurt her, she knew that. He had done this for her and she appreciated the gesture. It was a typical Harry thing to do. He seemed to know more about what she needed than she did herself.

A riding hat was perched on the horse's saddle. Emma picked it up and fitted it to her head. Harry grinned and cupped his hands giving her a leg up onto her horse before he swung himself easily into his own saddle and slapped his cattleman's hat onto his head.

In single file they headed into the bush. They didn't talk, the only sounds being the sounds of the horses' feet as they trod on the occasional stone and the sounds of the bush—buzzing flies, chattering parrots and the odd small reptile scurrying through the undergrowth.

Emma found herself gradually relaxing as they rode in silence through the bush. It felt strange to be riding again but enjoyable, and she was glad she was doing this with Harry. It would be a nice memory to keep.

By the time Harry stopped his horse at the top of a rocky peak Emma had found her rhythm. She brought her horse to a stop alongside Harry. He dismounted before helping her down and leading her to a flat boulder. It was warm from the afternoon sun and made a perfect lookout. She could see across the plains to the north. The countryside stretched away from them, there was a large lake in the distance but nothing man-made. Nothing but what Mother Nature had created. There was nothing to distract her, except for Harry, of course.

'Are you ready to talk about it?'

She closed her eyes and leant back against his chest. He was solid and reassuring and she had that now familiar feeling that nothing would go wrong while he was in her life. He was a man who could be trusted. She knew that.

'Why don't you start with the negatives?' he said.

She sighed. There were a lot of those. 'It means moving half way around the world.'

'Yes. That might take some planning to pull off. Not your strong point.' She could hear Harry smiling. 'But if it's something you really want, it'd be worth it.'

'I've never stayed in one place for more than three years. It's a huge undertaking to move my entire life, especially if it's only temporary.'

'It doesn't need to be temporary.'

Could she make the commitment? She didn't know. 'I can't imagine staying somewhere for ever. I've never done that before. And my family is in the UK.'

'Not all of them,' he argued. 'You're half-Australian and Sophie is here. And her family, your mother's family, are in Sydney.'

'It's not just where the job is, it's what it is,' she tried to explain. 'I love nursing, and I'm glad that this has given me the opportunity to get back into it, but maybe I'm better suited to an emergency department.'

'Why do you say that?'

'Yesterday, with Jess and Sam, was really difficult. I know I don't know Sam well at all and I'd never met Jess but because of their connection to you it made it really personal. I imagine that after doing this job for a while you'd get to know a lot of people and I'm not sure how I'd cope if we lost someone. It really hit home how far people are from medical help and we can't expect to save everyone. I don't know if I could handle that side of the job.'

'You must have lost people in hospital emergency departments.'

'Yes, but it's so much more personal out here. We're talking about people's family or friends or neighbours. There's more at stake.'

'That's probably why you're such a fabulous nurse—because you care about people.'

'You think I'm a good nurse?'

'I do. You've coped brilliantly with this job. I know it's not easy. I also know I'm not the only one who thinks you've done well. You wouldn't have been offered the job if the doctors didn't think you were up to it.'

'What do you mean?'

'The doctors would have recommended you. You have to be highly skilled to work out here and they wouldn't put your name forward unless they thought you were up to it.'

'Thank you. That's good to know but even if I decide to stay I'd have to leave the country and then come back, and I think Irene wants me to start immediately. My tourist visa expires soon. I'd have to apply for a working visa or Australian citizenship but I can't do that from here.' Emma knew the technicalities were irrelevant. She had one decision to make. Stay or go.

What she needed to do was decide if she would stay if Harry wasn't around.

She knew the answer was no. He was the only reason she would stay. She got the sense that she belonged, not to Outback Australia but to him.

She was considering Irene's offer based on Harry but that was foolish. She was imagining he was the one for her but he'd given her no indication that she was the one for him. She needed a better reason than that to stay.

She didn't need to go riding to get her answer.

She didn't need to gaze into the distance to find it. She already had it.

Unless Harry asked her to stay, she would go home.

'I can think of another way you can stay,' he said.

'How?'

'You could get married.'

Emma laughed. 'To whom?'

'Me.'

Emma's heart leapt in her chest and she could feel it beating a rapid tattoo against her ribs. She was taken completely by surprise. This was not the sort of suggestion she would expect to hear from a meticulous man who loved to plan things. 'You want to get married?'

'Well, one day,' he replied.

'But not right now?'

'I wasn't planning on it but if it will help you...'

Emma's heart plummeted, colliding heavily with her stomach. This was not how she'd ever imagined being proposed to. She shook her head. A marriage of convenience was not her idea of matrimonial bliss.

'I appreciate the thought but marriage is about two people who are in love wanting to spend the rest of their lives together. That's the only way I'm going to get married.' She paused as she tried to squash the swell of disappointment that was rushing through her because his proposal wasn't what she needed. 'Just out of curiosity, "one day" means when exactly?'

'When I have something to offer.'

She frowned. 'Like what?'

'My cattle station.'

'So not when you find the right girl and fall madly in love?'

'Finding the right partner for station life is harder than you might imagine.'

'Lucas found Jess.'

'He didn't have to look far. The three of us grew up together. Jess was our head stockman's daughter and Lucas and I have known her all our lives. She's the perfect station wife.'

'And Lucas got her too.'

'I don't want Jess,' Harry protested. 'She's the perfect station wife *for Lucas*. She's like a sister to me. I admit I'd like to find someone with some of her qualities but I don't want her and until I have a station of my own there's not much point looking for a wife.'

'So why would you marry me?'

'I told you. It would solve your problem. You'd be able to stay.'

'Getting a visa is not my problem. Working out what I want is my problem. I have more idea about what I don't want than what I do.'

'What don't you want?'

'I don't want to get married so that I can work. And I don't want to ruin your plans. I know your goal is to work hard, save money and buy Cooper Creek Station, it's not to get married. I appreciate the offer but it's not what either of us need. I don't want to be responsible for making your plans go awry. I've done enough of that in my own life.'

She would marry him in a flash if he said he loved her. But he hadn't. And anyway what sort of person married someone they'd only known for five weeks? That would be crazy.

She couldn't marry him.

She was happier than she'd been for a long time, because

of Harry, but it was unfair to expect him to be responsible for her happiness. She needed to be happy on her own, she needed to find her own inner peace, that was why she'd come to Australia. To find what she needed. To find herself. But instead she'd found Harry.

But if he didn't feel the same way as her, she knew it couldn't last. If he didn't love her, it would all end in tears.

Her heart sat like a stone in her chest. She knew she'd left herself open to heartache. She'd known for weeks she was falling in love with him, despite knowing his reputation and despite her vows to herself not to get involved. She'd told herself it was just a holiday romance, not a relationship, but a proper relationship with Harry was her heart's true desire. She needed to put some distance between them before her heart was well and truly broken.

She couldn't marry him.

No matter how much she wanted to.

CHAPTER ELEVEN

LUCAS nodded at the beer that was sitting on the bar in front of Harry. 'Are you going to drink that or wait till it evaporates?'

When things hadn't gone quite the way he'd envisaged with Emma, Harry had persuaded Lucas to meet for a beer and a meal as an alternative to the hospital cafeteria food. The idea of going home to an empty house hadn't appealed to him but now that they were at the pub Harry found he didn't really have much of an appetite. Not for a veal parmigiana and not for the beer.

He picked up his glass and had a half-hearted sip as Lucas asked, 'What's on your mind?'

'I proposed to Emma.'

Lucas almost choked on his drink. 'Hell, I didn't realise it was quite that serious between you. What did she say?'

'She said no.' Harry pushed a few chips around his plate. 'I can't say I blame her. It sort of came out of the blue.'

'How exactly do you propose to someone out of the blue?'

'She's been offered a job with the flying doctor service but she needs a working visa and to get that she has to leave the country. I thought if we got married she wouldn't need the visa and she wouldn't need to leave.'

'If that's how you worded your proposal, I'm not surprised she turned you down. Whatever happened to marrying for love? Women marry for love or money, you're offering her neither.' Lucas had finished his meal but he reached across and pinched some of Harry's chips as he asked. 'Do you love her?'

'I'm not ready to be in love.'

'What the hell is that supposed to mean? You can't plan falling in love. It just happens.'

'I always thought I'd be settled and *then* I'd get married.'

'Things don't always turn out how you planned. Did you propose because she wants to stay or because you want her to stay?'

'I think if she leaves it's very unlikely that she'll come back. And I don't want her to go.'

'But not wanting her to go isn't the same thing as wanting to marry her,' Lucas said. 'Ask yourself this. Can you imagine your life without Emma? Can you imagine her as the mother of your children? Can you imagine her by your side when you're eighty years old?'

Harry didn't know when he'd have a place to call his own but he knew that he wanted Emma with him whenever it was. He couldn't imagine his life without her in it. 'I can.'

'Just because your grand plan was to have Cooper Creek and then get married doesn't mean it has to happen that way. Don't let her go because of timing. You will get Cooper Creek one day and when you do you'll need the right woman by your side. Marriage isn't easy but I imagine it'd be a whole lot worse if you marry the wrong woman.'

Harry knew that Emma was the right woman for him. She was everything he'd imagined. She was everything he needed. She was beautiful, she was capable, she was intelligent and she was strong enough for Outback life. With Emma beside him he knew he could achieve anything.

'Propose because you can't bear the idea of her leaving,

not because it's easier for her to get a job this way. Don't pretend that's it's convenient, or that you're doing it as a favour to her.' Lucas was still giving advice.

'Ask her to marry you because you love her and you don't want to live without her. Be romantic. Be honest. Convince her that marrying you will be the best decision she'll ever make. Propose again but do it properly. What have you got to lose?'

For the first time in his life Harry felt like he had a lot to lose. He had *everything* to lose.

But Lucas was right. He had to do something because if he did nothing, Emma would leave.

He didn't know if he'd be able to convince her to stay but he had to try.

But what if he wasn't up to the challenge? Proposing to help her out was one thing. Proposing because he loved her was something else altogether. What if she left anyway?

Self-doubt was an unfamiliar experience for him. But he didn't know what he was more afraid of, admitting he loved her or having her leave. Which was more frightening?

The idea of her returning to the UK, of her leaving his life for ever was something he didn't want to contemplate.

And that realisation gave him his answer. He loved her. He didn't want to live without her. If he had to choose between Cooper Creek Station and Emma, he would choose Emma.

But he didn't expect to have to make that choice, and he certainly hadn't expected to make it now, but a phone call from Sam Cooper further complicated matters. And more complications were not what he needed.

Harry could sense his plans for the future unravelling. He had two problems, neither of which could be solved simply by good planning. Things were spiralling out of control. He had too many balls in the air and it was only a matter of time before some came crashing down.

He spent days looking at his options, but they were limited and he didn't have the luxury of time. Both problems came with deadlines that were fast approaching.

He needed help. He needed Lucas. He was reluctant to ask but he couldn't see another way out.

He got his chance when Lucas brought Jess back to town for a follow-up doctor's appointment. He invited them for dinner and as they ate he tried to put aside his feelings of guilt for what he was about to ask.

'I had a call from Sam Cooper a few days ago,' he said.

'How's he doing?' Jess asked. They all knew he was still in Adelaide, where he was recuperating from heart surgery.

'He's recovering well but he's talking about retiring,' Harry said. 'He's worried about coping with the physical side of the station and Jo's been in his ear about moving to Tamworth to be closer to their grandchildren.'

'He's ready to sell Cooper Creek?' Lucas asked.

'That's fantastic.' Jess was beaming. 'Congratulations.'

'How much?' Lucas asked.

That was the crux of the matter. The price. It was too much. Too much for him right now.

Harry told him and Lucas whistled in surprise. 'Have you got the money?'

Harry shook his head. 'Not enough to buy him out. Not yet. The bank will lend me some but there's still a shortfall.'

'Of?'

'Half a million.' Harry saw the raised eyebrows but he had to press on. He had to ask. 'What are the Connor's Corner finances like?'

'You're asking if I can lend you the money?'

Harry nodded. He hated asking but he needed Lucas. He couldn't do any of this without his help.

'Harry, there's nothing spare. You know we're restocking after three years of drought conditions. The money's gone. I'm sorry.'

He wasn't surprised. He'd known it was a long shot. It wasn't often they had spare cash floating around, it was almost always allocated to one project or another.

'Let me sleep on it,' Lucas said as Jess tried to stifle a yawn. 'We'll work something out,' he added as he hugged Harry goodnight.

But Harry wasn't sure there was anything Lucas could do. He either had the money or he didn't.

He was about to lose everything. Without Lucas's money Cooper Creek Station was out of reach and in a few days Emma would be gone. He didn't want her to go. He loved her. But he had no idea if she loved him. She'd been avoiding him since his disastrous proposal. She'd probably decided that he was completely mad and she'd do well to steer clear of him.

But what had Lucas said? Love or money. What if he could still offer both?

He could only think of one other option given his limited time frame. He'd have to talk to Sam but what if he could pull it off? The odds weren't greatly in his favour, but he had to try. He had one last chance.

He would talk to Sam. And then he'd talk to Emma. He just hoped she would listen.

Emma couldn't believe she had less than forty-eight hours left until she said goodbye to Broken Hill and the Australian Outback. To Grace and Irene. To Sophie and Mark. To Harry.

Somehow she'd made it through the past two weeks

when all she'd wanted to do was run away and hide. To go somewhere quiet and lick her wounds in private. To pretend she hadn't fallen in love. But she couldn't keep running away. Sophie had begged her to stay until her visa ran out and Emma knew that leaving early would leave the flying doctors short-staffed with Lisa still out of action so she agreed to stay. But she requested different shifts from Harry. She couldn't bear to see him daily and have a constant reminder of all she was about to lose.

She had made her decision to return to England, not because she couldn't live here but because she couldn't live here without Harry. She'd live anywhere if Harry was with her. If Harry loved her. But it didn't look like that would happen. Her flight home was booked and Harry had never asked her to stay. Not properly. At least, not the way she wanted.

Sophie's house was bursting at the seams with all the people Emma had met since she'd arrived in the Hill. So many of them, who she now called friends, but there was one person she'd miss above all.

The air around her vibrated. He was behind her. She could feel him. She could smell him. She wanted to turn around and bury her face in his chest but she held herself in check. She'd missed him terribly over the past two weeks and she couldn't imagine how she was going to feel when she was gone, when he was gone from her life and she knew she would never see him again. She wanted to turn around and throw her arms around his neck and kiss him senseless, but she couldn't give in. It was over even if it hadn't sunk in yet that this was the end.

'So, you're really leaving.' His deep voice resonated through her. She closed her eyes and let it wash over her before she turned round.

She nodded.

Harry reached for her. His hands brushed her upper arms, running from her shoulders to her elbows, sending little lightning bolts to her groin. She knew she should step away, out of reach, but lust and longing had her frozen in place.

His bright blue eyes locked with hers. 'I have a favour to ask you,' he said. 'Will you spend the day with me tomorrow?'

'It's my last day.'

'I know. And I can't quite believe you're leaving. I know you didn't want to marry me but I thought I might be able to persuade you to spend one last day together.'

'You never asked me to marry you.'

'Yes, I did.'

Emma shook her head. She could remember that conversation word for word. 'No, you didn't. You said we could get married, that's not the same thing at all.'

Harry gave her a half-smile. He looked sad. She couldn't remember him ever looking sad.

'We can argue about semantics tomorrow,' he told her. 'Please say you'll spend the day with me.'

Emma knew she should refuse. It would only make things worse. It would only make it harder to leave. But she couldn't do it. She couldn't deprive herself of the final moments. Lisa and Irene were heading towards her and she knew they were about to be interrupted. She also knew she'd probably regret the decision but she was nodding her head anyway. She would spend her final day with Harry.

It was almost like old times, Emma thought as she sat in the co-pilot's seat. As a favour to Sam, Harry had offered to fly out to Cooper Creek Station and check on the place, and Emma was going with him.

This time tomorrow she'd be on another plane, bound

for England, and she'd never see Harry again. She knew her heart would be breaking but there was nothing she could do. All she could do was make the most of today. She'd arrived in Australia miserable and she'd be leaving even more so, but at least she'd been happy while she'd been here.

The plane touched down on the dirt airstrip. As usual Harry pulled off a smooth landing but Emma was surprised to find that no one was waiting to greet them. She was used to seeing at least a few welcoming faces whenever they arrived on the cattle stations.

'Where is everyone?' she asked.

'There's a rodeo in Thargomindah,' he explained. 'Most of the staff have gone into town for the weekend.'

Harry took her hand as they walked down to the house. His fingers were warm and Emma felt the familiar flutter of excitement flow through her with his touch. She was going to miss him so much. Her life had been changed for ever since meeting him and she knew she wouldn't get over him in a hurry. If ever.

She let her gaze roam over the house as they got nearer. Last time she'd been here it had been to treat and evacuate Sam. It had been dark and, even if it hadn't, she'd been too busy to take note of the surroundings. The house was a sprawling building, constructed of weatherboard and elevated on stilts, encased by a wide veranda. A large expanse of lawn ran away from the house and sloped down to the edge of the Cooper Creek.

One of Sam's stockman was waiting at the bottom of the steps. Emma recognised him from the gymkhana at Innamincka.

'G'day, boss,' he greeted Harry as he shook his hand.

'Jonno,' Harry replied. 'You remember Emma?'

Jonno dipped his hat.

'How're things?' Harry asked.

'All good. No dramas. Everything's set.'

'Great. Thanks, mate.'

Harry still had hold of her hand and he led her up the steps as Jonno took off across the dirt.

'Boss?' Emma asked as Harry took her round to the front of the house. Jonno's greeting hadn't gone unnoticed by her but it made no sense.

Harry stopped in the middle of the veranda beside an enormous wooden table. It was set for two and there was a bottle of champagne chilling in a wine cooler in the centre. 'I'll explain,' he said as he pulled a chair out for her and waited for her to sit down.

'Sam and I have come to an arrangement. You are looking at the new owner of Cooper Creek Station.'

He was grinning from ear to ear and Emma thought her heart would explode with happiness for him. He'd done it. He'd made his dream come true.

'Harry! Congratulations!' She sprang from her chair and launched herself into his lap, throwing her arms around his neck. She kissed him. 'I'm so happy for you. I didn't realise your dream was this close. I thought you couldn't afford it yet.'

'I can't afford it on my own but I had to have it. Sam and I have formed a partnership. I'll make repayments and share profits with him until I've cleared the loan. But...' Harry checked his watch and gestured across the lawn towards the river '...as of half an hour ago, this is all mine.'

'So that's what the champagne is for? We're celebrating?' She hadn't thought she could feel like celebrating on today of all days but she was truly happy for Harry. This was everything he'd wanted.

'Almost.'

'What else is there? You've done it. You've achieved your dream.'

'Only part one.'

'What's part two?' she asked.

'Convincing you to stay. I want you to stay here. With me.'

'I don't know anything about working on a cattle station.'

'I'll teach you.'

Why had he left it until the last minute? To have him ask her to stay was what she'd been waiting for, hoping for. But she needed more. He hadn't said he loved her and she knew that was what she needed to hear. If he didn't love her, there was no point in staying.

'Harry, I leave tomorrow. My flight is booked. My visa is expiring. If I don't leave I'll be deported. I have to go.'

'But I want you to stay.'

'We've had this conversation.'

'Not exactly,' he said. 'Do you think you could live out here? You once told me that you thought it was beautiful out in the bush. Peaceful, idyllic. Do you think you could be happy here? We wouldn't be able to pack up and move every few years. You'd be here for the long haul.'

'What would I do?'

'I can teach you everything you need to know and if you wanted to you could still work for the flying doctor service. You could do a couple of shifts a week or a fortnight, stay in town overnight. You could have it all, Em. I can give it to you.'

'You've got it all figured out, haven't you?'

Harry shrugged and gave her a half-smile. 'I'm a planner. I figure one of us has to be. The only thing I haven't figured out is whether you'll agree to stay. Owning a cattle station is my dream. I know it's not yours, but I don't want to be here without you. I need you. What do you think?'

'I don't know—'

'Wait.' He put a finger on her lips, stopping her from finishing her sentence. He gathered her to his chest and stood up, placing her back onto his seat and kneeling in front of her on one knee.

He took her hands in his. 'Emma Matheson, this is me, asking you properly and as nicely as I know how, to be my wife. I want to share my dream with you. I want to share my future with you. I want to share my life with you. I love you, Em. Will you please marry me?'

Emma burst into tears. She tried to maintain her composure but it was all so overwhelming.

'Emma! What's wrong?'

'I can't remember the last time someone said they loved me,' she sniffed.

Harry laughed and the circumstances reminded her of the day she'd met him, the first time he'd laughed at her expense and how she hadn't minded a bit. How she'd thought he was gorgeous. To think that was only a few short weeks ago. She couldn't believe she'd only known him for a couple of months.

'If you agree to be my wife, I promise I will tell you I love you every day for the rest of our lives.'

Harry reached into his pocket and pulled out a small box. He opened the lid to reveal an opal nestled on black velvet. 'Tony found this when he was removing the rubble from the tunnel collapse. It turns out there was still some opal there after all. He polished it up and I bought it for you. This symbolises the moment I realised I couldn't lose you.'

'You've known for all that time? Why didn't you tell me then?'

'I knew I couldn't lose you that day but I didn't realise then I couldn't lose you for ever. For so long I'd been set on getting this station and when I finally managed to sort that out I realised that there was one thing more important to me than this land and that's you. And I was about to lose you for good. I don't want that to happen. My dream won't be complete without you. I love you, Emma. Do you love me?'

She nodded and she could feel more tears threatening to spill onto her cheeks but they were tears of joy. 'Yes. I do. I feel I belong with you. From the moment I first saw you I've been drawn to you. I feel like we are two opposite ends of a magnet. You're impossible for me to resist. I know I belong with you but I can't stay. I have to leave.'

Less than an hour earlier she'd thought it was going to be difficult to make herself get on the plane tomorrow, now it would be almost impossible.

'I know, believe me, I know. But you can come back. I'll be waiting for you. Please say you'll come back to me. Please say you'll be my wife.'

'Of course I'll come back and marry you,' she said as she pulled him to his feet and kissed him as if her life depended on it. 'You are the love of my life.'

EPILOGUE

EMMA was woken by squawking galahs in a tree outside her bedroom. She opened her eyes, momentarily disoriented before she remembered that she was back on Cooper Creek Station. She was home and today was her wedding day.

She'd been back in Australia for just over a month, living with Harry, but she was still amazed every day that this was her new home. Life was chaotic, there was so much to learn, but there was never a dull moment and she was happy, blissfully happy, with her new life and with Harry.

She wondered where he was right now, what he was doing. She'd made him sleep in another room last night, telling him it was wedding-eve protocol, but she'd missed him. The bed had felt too big and cold and lonely and she'd spent the night wishing she hadn't banished him. After today she planned on spending as many nights together as possible. If she was going to town to do shifts with the flying doctors, she planned on taking him with her. She smiled to herself. How things had changed. Not only was she now an Australian who was about to get married to the love of her life, she was now also planning on making plans.

Harry stuck his head into her room. Their room. 'Good morning.' He was smiling from ear to ear and she couldn't help but smile back at him. She was always happy when he was around.

'Hey, you're not supposed to see me before the wedding,' she teased.

'We're not getting married for hours. If you think I'm going to wait all day, you don't know me very well,' he said as he came into the room.

The fact that Harry was bucking tradition shouldn't have surprised her. Nothing about today was going to be traditional. The station was overflowing with wedding guests, people had been arriving for the past few days and many would be staying for a day or two after the wedding.

Sophie and her family were here and Sam and Jo were visiting from Tamworth. Emma wondered if they found it strange to have new people living in their house but they seemed happy with the changes, her stepmother and half-sisters had arrived from England and Emma was enjoying introducing them to Australian life. And Irene, Grace and the majority of the flying doctor team were due today.

'Can I steal you away for half an hour? There's something I want to show you.'

Emma dressed quickly, picking her hat up as she left the house. Slapping a hat on her head had become second nature out here under the harsh sun. She followed Harry outside, surprised at how quiet the house and yards were.

'Where is everyone?' she asked him.

'It's only six o'clock. Lots are still sleeping and the ones who are awake are in the staff kitchen.'

Emma could smell bacon frying as she followed Harry past the staff quarters. The cook would be kept busy for the next few days catering for the guests. Harry kept walking past the kitchen and up towards the stables.

'Where are we going?'

'You'll see.'

Harry stopped beside the railings in the mounting yard. A pretty chestnut mare with a white blaze was loose in the yard but she quickly came to Harry's side when she saw the apple in his hand.

Harry handed Emma the apple and she held it out to the mare, who took it gently from her hand with soft, velvet lips. Emma didn't recognise the horse. 'She's a beautiful horse, who does she belong to?'

'You. She's my wedding gift to you.'

'Really?' Emma threw her arms around Harry and kissed him. 'Thank you, she's gorgeous.'

'Shall we go for a ride?'

'I would love to but I'm not sure if I should.'

'I promise I'll have you back in plenty of time. I'm not going to miss my own wedding.'

'It's not that. I have a wedding present for you too.' Emma took Harry's hand and placed it on her stomach. His hand was warm and Emma felt the now familiar flutter of excitement in her belly at his touch. 'We're going to have a baby.'

'You're pregnant?'

Emma nodded.

'What? When?'

'I think it was that night out in the billabong, when we spent the weekend in Innamincka.' She grinned at him. 'I told you it was a magical spot.'

Harry scooped her up, lifting her off her feet. 'This is brilliant, the best day ever,' he said as he kissed her thoroughly.

'You're happy?' Emma asked as she wrapped her legs around his waist and held onto him.

'I couldn't be happier,' he replied, before he kissed her again. 'I have everything I want right here.'

The mare whinnied softly and Emma laughed. Her life was fabulous. 'I love you, Harry Connor, let's go and get married.'

* * * * *

Mills & Boon® Online

Discover more romance at
www.millsandboon.co.uk

- 🌹 **FREE** online reads

- 🌹 **Books** up to one
  month before shops

- 🌹 **Browse our books**
  before you buy

  ...and much more!

For exclusive competitions and instant updates:

 Like us on **facebook.com/romancehq**

 Follow us on **twitter.com/millsandboonuk**

 Join us on **community.millsandboon.co.uk**

Visit us Online Sign up for our FREE eNewsletter at
www.millsandboon.co.uk

WEB/M&B/RTL4

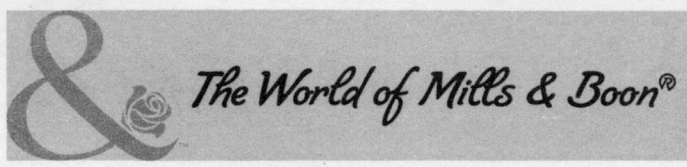

What will you treat yourself to next?

Ignite your imagination,
step into the past...
6 new stories every month

INTRIGUE...

Breathtaking romantic suspense
Up to 8 new stories every month

Medical Romance

Captivating medical drama –
with heart
6 new stories every month

MODERN™

International affairs,
seduction & passion guaranteed
9 new stories every month

nocturne™

Deliciously wicked
paranormal romance
Up to 4 new stories every month

RIVA™

Live life to the full –
give in to temptation
3 new stories every month available
exclusively via our Book Club